A DIFFERENT KIND
OF MADNESS

A DIFFERENT KIND OF MADNESS

Pauline Schokman

SPHINX

First published in 2019 by Sphinx, an imprint of
Aeon Books Ltd
12 New College Parade
Finchley Road
London NW3 5EP

British Library Cataloguing in Publication Data

A C.I.P. for this book is available from the British Library

ISBN-13: 978-1-91257-316-5

Typeset by Medlar Publishing Solutions Pvt Ltd, India

Printed in Great Britain
by TJ International Ltd, Padstow, Cornwall

www.aeonbooks.co.uk

www.sphinxbooks.co.uk

For

A. R.

CHAPTER ONE

Colombo, Friday 25th September 1964

Greta van Buuren entered the room and glared with sudden irritation at her daughter and her child's ayah as they sat on the floor opposite each other. They were consumed by a complex game involving a group of small colourful cloth dolls. "You two will have to leave, now! Just go somewhere else!"

They glanced up at her, their faces wearing identical expressions of surprise, swiftly followed by concern. Greta's annoyance grew.

"Yes, Madam." Charlotte's deep brown eyes briefly met the intense blue-green gaze of her mistress, then glanced away. Both women were of a similar age, in their mid-twenties. Greta was the shorter of the two, petite and shapely, while Charlotte was slender and erect in her crisp white blouse and multi-coloured sarong, as she stood and attempted to placate her mistress. She began arranging the little dolls on the top shelf of a low bamboo bookcase, where they usually resided. Leila was immediately by her side helping, leaning into her as they worked together.

"The tailor will be here any minute and he'll be using the drawing room. I need this room to do my accounts." Greta gave a quick twitch of her head. Why was she justifying her actions to a servant? Charlotte's presence, which she had simply taken for granted since her daughter's birth, had recently begun to irk her. She now found the other woman's quiet, persistently kind and calming manner cloying, and as for Leila standing there, pasting herself against the servant's body. "Come here, Leila."

The little girl crossed the room tentatively and stood in front of her mother.

"Well? Have you gone mute? Good morning, Leila!"

"Good morning, Mummy." Her mother had slept in that morning and she'd had breakfast with Daddy at the dining table, rather than with Charlotte and the servants in the kitchen. The little girl stood in front of her mother, unsure what would follow. She knew she always had to be quiet around her mother, so as not to annoy her, but it was clear that Mummy was not in a good mood today. Leila tried even harder, standing as still as she could. She gazed up at the beautiful face and the harsh gaze that confronted her.

Greta bent down and pecked at her daughter's cheek. It was what was required. It was what a mother did. "Well, off you go then."

She had no desire to give them more thought. Her preoccupation with her dress returned. It must be a success. She had found the perfect Vogue design and a bolt of emerald silk. The Leembruggens always threw the most amazing parties and the party tonight had an air of mystery about it. Some announcement would be made. She was sure of it. She imagined her entrance and the admiration that would greet her. She looked up at her child and the ayah who were just leaving the large family room to head out along the long veranda that led down to the kitchen and servants' quarters. "Your grandmother will be here at ten, Leila. Be sure you're in a clean dress."

It was stunningly new. Until now that information would have been communicated to Charlotte in a straightforward, even way. Leila looked from her mother to her ayah in confusion. Charlotte took the little girl's hand and they kept walking. "As you wish, Madam."

2

She did not turn to address her mistress. The comment was made as she and the child continued to walk away. She knew her days as an ayah here were numbered. She had known it at the child's fourth birthday, only a few weeks ago. She and Leila had cuddled and laughed together as was their custom, but something very different had been turned their way; a look from her mistress that held both jealousy and loathing. Charlotte had sensed then that her mistress was not even fully aware of it. She had been the child's ayah since her birth. How could a four year old deal with this woman, this unnatural mother who had no love for her only child? She shivered inwardly. She would no longer be here to protect the little one.

The coolness of early morning was already gone and the bright rays of tropical sunlight intensified the rich greens of the garden foliage that flanked the veranda. A sunbird darted past a giant yellow hibiscus flower rimmed with burnt orange. The iridescent blue at the bird's throat caught Leila's attention and she tugged at Charlotte's hand, stopping to watch the little bird as it flew further into the garden. A grey squirrel ran along the veranda's edge and halted not far from her feet. She watched as the small animal cleaned its front paws, unperturbed by her presence. She laughed with delight, then her face clouded.

Her ayah looked at her and smiled gently. "What, raththaran baba? What worries you this auspicious morning?"

Leila laughed a musical laugh. "Oh Charlotte, you think every morning is auspicious!"

"It must be so, when we are together, when we can play. Do you not think?"

"I was remembering that baby squirrel, you know the one we saw last monsoon time, that was washed out of its nest and got drowned in the drain." Leila closed her eyes and tried to remember the wonderful silence that enveloped everything when she stood just here on the veranda in the midst of curtains of monsoon rain, and the smell of the rain. It was much

3

better than thinking about the dead nude baby squirrel swirling in the eddies of the fast-running drain water.

There was a harsh repetitive metallic sound and Charlotte pulled at Leila's hand, indicating it was time they moved on. Leila looked up at her quizzically.

"Come, we must go. Jason is here." Charlotte shook her head and clucked her tongue as they walked on past the area of garden where Jason was working with his shears to trim back a large bush.

"You don't like Jason, do you Charlotte?"

"Jason likes his arrack too much. He should not be here. Come."

Leila did not understand what that meant, but she hurried to keep pace. Charlotte liked most people. She was funny and playful and kind, but she had never liked Jason. It was a good thing that he only came one morning a week, and didn't live in the servants' quarters with Charlotte and Rani the cook, and Harold the servant boy who also drove Mummy around sometimes.

They were almost at the kitchen and Harold was there husking coconuts on a metal spike by the open door. Leila dropped Charlotte's hand and ran to squat in front of him and watch him at work while Charlotte headed on into the kitchen. Leila thought Harold was wonderful. He was nineteen years old with laughing eyes and a keen sense of fun that all the females who frequented the kitchen and servants' quarters enjoyed immensely. He had once made her a beautiful crepe-paper kite, stretching the green and pink paper carefully and attaching it to a bamboo frame. He had even let her tie on the tail. She had taken it to Galle Face Green with Mummy and Daddy and had flown it so high.

"Can I try, Harold?"

Harold spoke kindly. "No, Little Missy. Not today. As you see, I have many to do."

Leila looked at the pile of coconuts next to Harold and replied in her most thoughtful voice. "Yes, Harold, I can see how much work you have."

He suppressed a smile and continued his work.

Leila made her way into the kitchen. It was a large room with a long central bench. She often headed here if she woke too early in the morning. It was on the way to Charlotte's room, and if Charlotte was not already up, or if something in the kitchen smelt especially good, Leila would stop here instead and sit on her haunches next to Rani, waiting for Charlotte. She'd watch as Rani pounded the spices for the day's cooking in the large stone mortar. When she felt the time had come to rouse Charlotte she would creep as quietly as she could to Charlotte's room, hoping to surprise her. Somehow, she never did. She would most often find Charlotte sitting on the woven mat that served as her bed and brushing her long hair.

Leila loved Charlotte's room. Like all the rooms in the servants' quarters it was small and dark and had no windows. It was completely different to any of the rooms in the main house. But it was the only dark place anywhere that didn't frighten her. It smelled of Charlotte and Charlotte smelled of sandalwood and of the coconut oil she used on her hair. Her sarong and blouse were always crisp and fresh and her dark hair and skin gleamed like her eyes. Leila always felt safe when she was with Charlotte.

Today Rani was mixing flour and coconut dough, kneading the mixture on the bench then returning it to the bowl, adding more flour or more milk, repeating the process again and again until she was perfectly happy with the consistency. This meant she was making rotis for lunch. Maybe because Gran was coming and she loved rotis. Charlotte must have told Rani. Mummy never thought about such things. Rani sometimes let Leila shape the dough into little balls and pat them into the small flat circles she would then fry. On the bench coconut

5

sambal and chutneys were ready to be served. Rani looked up at Leila and smiled at her; she tipped her head in the direction of a little dish at the far end of the bench. Leila didn't need a second invitation. She reached in and popped a small square of the sweet caramel flavoured milk toffee into her mouth.

Rani and Charlotte went on with their long conversation about each of their mothers in Sinhalese. Leila knew that the servants had been told by Mummy to talk to her in English, but that didn't stop them talking to each other in Sinhalese when she was around. Leila loved the lilting sound of the Sinhalese language and the wonderful things that Charlotte and Rani and Harold discussed: stories about each of their different homes. Rani had a big family with lots of little brothers and sisters who lived in Colombo. She went to visit them whenever she could. Harold's and Charlotte's families both lived far away and they only went to visit at special times of year like Vesak. Harold came from a village by the sea. He could climb up a coconut tree as fast as anything. He knew everything about fishermen and how they made their huts and nets. Charlotte came from a village near the jungle and Leila loved her stories best of all, especially the ones about monkeys and all the playful, naughty things they did.

Leila heard a strange loud squawking going on outside and rushed out to see what was happening just as Harold cut the head off a chicken. A torrent of blood spurted like a fountain from the headless body running at her. Leila shrieked and ran up the path. She was terrified of the chicken.

"Come back, Little Missy!" Harold called after her with concern, but then turned rapidly to his task of catching and cleaning the chicken.

Leila stopped. Her head was spinning. The sound of Jason's shears halted abruptly. She could feel him near her and smell the awful smell he had on his breath. She felt a hand grip her shoulder tightly.

"Pretty Little Missy."

"Do not touch her! Eyata yanna denna!" Charlotte pulled Leila to her side and glowered fiercely at the gardener. He sneered at her, but retreated wordlessly and moved away. Soon he was hard at work again, with no sign that anything untoward had occurred at all. Leila clung to her ayah's body. Charlotte stroked her hair until she stopped trembling then moved gently away from her and cupped Leila's face in her hand, tilting her head upwards. "Come, little one, we must go to the house, change your dress, now. Your grandmother be here very soon."

They walked slowly towards the main house. Charlotte wished she could appeal to someone. Jason was a most unsuitable person to have working in a house with a young child. Even she and Rani felt his menace. Perhaps the master might listen if she could find a time to speak to him alone. The master was a kind man. Yet, what was she thinking? When would such a time ever come? She never saw the master alone. He was most often preoccupied with his work and seemed unwilling to acknowledge the awful truth of his wife's behaviour to their child. How then would he see danger from a servant? It was also rumoured that Jason was the son of the master's own ayah. Better that she kept silent.

They were just rounding the side of the house and about to head for Leila's bedroom when Greta noticed them from the back drawing room. Charlotte saw the anger in her mistress's eyes and drew it towards herself. "Madam, I take Leila to change for her grandmother's visit."

Greta motioned Leila towards her and turned her around. She gasped loudly when she saw the myriad spots of blood on the back of the little girl's dress.

"There was a chicken with blood and no head Mummy ..."

Charlotte intervened quickly. "Harold kill ..."

Greta held up her hand. "Just change her, then wash the dress! Now!"

Charlotte simply nodded and led Leila away. Once in the child's bedroom she quickly helped Leila undress and searched

7

in her wardrobe for her new party dress which had blue and white stripes and round buttons with seahorses imprinted on them. The little girl loved the dress and it might help cheer her. Leila touched her ayah gently on the shoulder as she bent to button the dress. "What's the matter, Charlotte? Why is Mummy cross with you and not me? You're not a dhobi. You never have to wash my clothes!"

"You wash blood away quickly and it leaves no stain. That is what your mother is thinking, I am certain. Come, I hear voices. It is your grandmother." She smiled at Leila and kissed her on the top of her head as she pushed her gently towards the door of the room. "Go, I will see you later." Leila was not convinced, but the distraction worked, and she ran away excitedly for she adored her grandmother.

Charlotte stood still. She knew that Emma de Zylva would watch over her granddaughter. But how was she going to bear this change in her mistress? If Greta spoke to her this way in front of Rani or Harold how could she stay and abide the shame? She held back tears of rage and indignation. She was a proud woman. Something in her wished to simply leave, but she knew that this was what she was being driven to. No, she would stay for as long as she could. She must at least find a way to say goodbye properly before she left, or she would betray the child's trust and confidence in her.

Leila's cantering footsteps took her into the family room and straight to her grandmother, who stood on her own gazing out at the garden, her slender frame silhouetted against the bright sunlight. Leila nearly bowled Emma over as she flung herself at her and hugged her fiercely. Emma righted herself and cuddled the little girl who clung to her. "Oh, Leila darling, what a shock you gave me!"

They both burst into peals of laughter. Leila loved her grandmother's weekly visits; she loved her smile, the silvery streaks in her curly hair, the soft, soothing sound of her voice, she loved sitting on her lap and nestling into her, but most of all she loved her smell. Gran had her own smell that was fragrant and comforting. It was different to Charlotte's smell, but the same sense of safety came with it.

"Mummy's really busy today." Leila sighed deeply. "I think she's going to a party with Daddy tonight or something. The tailor came a while ago and Charlotte and I had to go away."

"Where is Charlotte?" Emma realised that it was the first time Charlotte had not been there to greet her together with Leila, although she usually left the two of them alone and then mysteriously reappeared at just the right moment to engage Leila in some form of play, so that Emma's leaving was made easy. Leila said nothing. She pouted and looked away. Emma decided not to pursue the matter further. "Why don't we go have a look at this dress?" Leila's eyes widened with excitement. She was seldom allowed anywhere near the tailor when he came to visit. He was an object of great fascination. Emma took her hand and they walked together into the sitting room.

Greta turned distractedly as her mother and daughter entered the room. She held a dress of green silk which was still in the making. She was suddenly alert. "Ah, Mum." She pulled the dress against her and looked at her mother with a sense of challenge. "So? Your expert opinion?" Her tone was half mocking, half urgent.

"It's beautiful, Greta. You'll look lovely in it."

Greta said nothing but relaxed visibly as she handed the dress back to the tailor. He adjusted his glasses, gathered the material before him and sat as a maestro at his instrument. Then his foot moved, the pedal surged and with it came a wild whirring that would ultimately produce something quite perfect. Greta watched him for a moment. The light caught her dark brown hair and it blazed auburn. She was petite, slender and shapely, with olive-brown skin and large, blue-green, almond-shaped eyes. She seemed totally unaware of the effect her beauty had on anyone who saw her, especially these two, though in a different place in herself she took it quite for granted.

She looked at her mother and daughter standing close, holding hands, at one with each other. "I'm glad you're here, Mum. Leila's been annoying me all morning. I really don't have the time!"

Leila stiffened with the unfairness of it. Her grandmother shot her an understanding and placating look, then turned to Greta. "That's fine, Greta, we have our plans. You finish whatever you're doing." She held Leila's hand more firmly and led her back to the family room with its space and light.

Immediately they entered the room Emma headed for the piano, sat down and began to play. Leila watched, mesmerised; there was something magical in her grandmother, she was sure of it. Her playing seemed like some kind of dance; her body moved to and fro, swayed and returned as her hands glided over the keys. Leila began to dance too, around the room and back again, not in creation of the music but in unison with it. The strains of Chopin finally stilled. Leila slipped onto her grandmother's lap and rested against her. Her breath came slowly, deeply, and she sighed. Her grandmother stroked her hair gently and sadness found them in their pleasure.

A pert step pulled them both back and brought Greta into the room. They noted immediately that she was in a good mood and the watchful tension that had roused in each of them at the sound of her step eased. The dress must still be progressing well. Greta moved to adjust the curtains. She spoke in a light distracted way. "I've invited Sylvie Kelly and her little boy Johann for lunch as well, Mum." She turned and looked at her mother pointedly, her tone suddenly harsh. "Please don't spend the entire meal talking about Cynthia! Sylvie is my friend now." Sylvia Kelly had been one of her sister Cynthia's best friends at school.

"Of course, I won't Greta. But I'll most certainly ask her if she's had any news from Cynthie. I haven't heard from her for three weeks."

"Imagine that! Three whole weeks! I haven't heard from her for months."

"Nonsense, you showed me the doll she sent Leila for her birthday."

"Yes, with a lovely card, and not so much as a line to me."

"She's so busy in Kent with the three boys and no servants. I'm sure it's a very different life there. And Ernest is away with work some of the time."

Greta turned and looked at her mother directly. "I never understood why you didn't go to England with them when they left, or later after she had the twins. She was always your favourite and I'm sure you could be a great help to her in her busy life." Her voice had a snide edge; she was seething with the jealousy that inevitably surfaced when the subject of her older sister entered any conversation.

Emma glanced towards Leila, who had hopped off her lap the moment Greta entered the room and was standing silently beside her.

Greta followed her glance and gave a short snort of contempt. "Oh, of course, never in front of the children!" She turned back to the curtains and made a show of adjusting them again. Neither her mother or daughter could see, or begin to imagine, the tears that had welled in her eyes, unbidden. When she turned back to them there was no trace of pain or vulnerability; her face wore the somewhat superior and condescending mask that she managed to muster for most interactions with other females. With men, she was quite different.

Emma was glad that this was how Greta interpreted her show of concern for Leila. Had Greta for a moment suspected that Emma continued to stay in Ceylon because of her love for her only granddaughter, and her guilt regarding her daughter's inability to love the child, who knew what might happen? She feared for her daughter's stability, and dreaded

11

that the harshness that was aimed at her granddaughter might turn to something far more vicious.

Certainly, since Greta had met and married Jeff van Buuren, the violent distress of her teens had seemed to evaporate. But Emma did not trust it, had seen this form of behaviour come and go in the past, in Greta's father. Then she had believed that weeks or months of more reasonable relating had to mean a permanent change, that the dark times were over. Always she had been proven wrong, had felt the pain of disappointment, gullibility, betrayal anew; each time with the same searing intensity. Certainly, his rages were louder, fuelled by alcohol and male aggression and more visible to anyone present. But she had no doubt that Greta could decimate her child's sense of self in a different way, quieter but every bit as penetrating.

In truth, she would have loved nothing more than to go to England with Cynthia when she and her husband had emigrated six years earlier, taking her only grandchild at that time, Jacob, who was a year old, with them. Cynthia loved her dearly, would have relished her help and companionship. She would have been appreciated. But Greta had just married Jeff after knowing him only a few months. Emma had feared leaving her brittle younger daughter alone, and had planned to join Cynthia once she was assured that Greta was settled in her marriage.

But Greta had soon been pregnant and become both volatile and unpredictable again. Emma had feared the worst, and yet, when catastrophe struck, two miscarriages in swift succession, Greta had somehow come through it all with amazing self-containment. Emma's guilt had begun to ease. It was Leila's birth that had brought the true catastrophe. Emma fell deeply in love with her granddaughter the moment she saw her, and realised immediately that Greta could not love her child, might even hate her.

Emma had found herself terrified then. For in some deeply superstitious part of herself, that she loathed, she feared that she had cursed her daughter; this was how she had felt about Greta at the time of her birth. It had been her life's work to find affection for her younger daughter. In addition, it went against everything in her to believe in the mere idea of curses; in the pervading superstitions that she had been taught belonged with the village people, or in the servants' quarters, not in a Presbyterian woman like herself, one of European heritage and custom. So, she had stayed in her island home, now caught in turmoil and racial unrest, at a time she might easily have left it. She mostly told herself she stayed to help her daughter, but somewhere she knew that she stayed to protect the granddaughter she loved.

Leila could see that something was very wrong between Gran and Mummy. Her grandmother's presence imbued courage. "Rani's making rotis instead of rice for lunch, Mummy. That's good, isn't it? 'Cause Johann loves rotis."

"Of course she's making rotis. I asked her to make rotis. I know what Johann likes." Each brief sentence was punctuated with a quiet rage that dared the little girl to be so bold as to speak again.

Emma stared at her daughter wordlessly. Greta fidgeted in irritation, then spoke to Leila in an altogether different way, a far lighter tone. "Why don't you run down and see how Rani's going, Leila? Tell her she'll need to set the dining table for five." She turned to her mother. "Sylvie insists that the children eat with us. I don't understand it, but she is the guest!"

Emma waited until Leila was well on her way towards the kitchen, then turned to her daughter. "What is it, Greta? What's bothering you today? I haven't seen you so on edge for a long time."

"Don't start on me! I know you're always watching, expecting me to make a mess of things. Or maybe hoping I will? But I'm doing just fine. Jeff loves me. My home is well run. I have friends now. I have my own life! I don't need your approval!"

13

"I didn't mean to upset you, Greta." Emma's tone was neutral, placating.

"There you go, talking as if I'm the one with the problem. You're just jealous because everything has worked out so well for me. We're much richer than Cynthia ever was." She looked at her mother pointedly. "I won't talk about you and your struggles of course."

"You can be very cruel." Emma looked her daughter directly in the eyes, her head high.

"Don't ask me where I learned the art." Greta had one eyebrow raised, her head was tilted to one side, her sneering half-smile robbed her of her beauty. In that instant, she was the image of her father.

"I don't need to, I remember all too clearly."

Emma realised that the conversation was veering in the opposite direction to the one she intended. It verged on the fights and rages she remembered from her daughter's teens; that would flare into a sudden litany of blame hurled her way for everything to do with Jürgen and his place, or absence, in their lives. She had no idea why Greta was so stirred up at present, but any concern from her was clearly unwanted and destined to be misconstrued or used as the focus of an attack. She racked her brain for a way to avert the growing conflict or divert the situation. Greta was expecting guests. She would never behave badly in front of Sylvia Kelly. This might be a way to steer her daughter away from confrontation.

"Come, Greta, won't your guests be here soon? You haven't told me why you've invited Sylvie, or for that matter, why the Leembruggens are throwing this huge party tonight?"

Greta, who had been pacing back and forth beside the curtains as her irritation with her mother grew, stopped. She stood still, then turned slowly to face Emma. "The two don't need to be related, do they?"

14

"I wasn't implying that at all." Emma struggled with her sense of exasperation. There appeared to be no way to have a more normal discussion.

Greta laughed unexpectedly. "But, of course they are related! I'm planning to see what I can get out of Sylvie." Her tone was suddenly excited, conspiratorial. "I'm sure the Leembruggens are going to make some announcement at the party tonight. I just hope they're not the next ones heading off overseas."

Emma hesitated, momentarily shocked at the rapid change in her daughter's mood even though she had hoped to engineer it. She hurriedly picked up the conversation. "Highly unlikely. Lester would never leave all his assets here. They should have left years ago, if they wanted to take their money with them."

Greta became solemn. She found the sense of impending doom that pervaded current Burgher society too difficult to think about. She looked at her mother plaintively. "I can't talk about this now. I'm going to check on the tailor. Play with Leila when she gets back, won't you, Mum?"

* * *

The front doorbell rang. Greta, who had been hovering around the tailor in preference to rejoining her mother and daughter, left him to his task and went to answer it. Moments later Sylvia Kelly bustled into the family room in her friendly energetic way with her boisterous little son in tow. Johann, who had walked quietly by his mother's side as she chatted with Greta on their way through the house, bolted for Leila the moment he saw her. He clutched an ebony box and, placing it on the couch before her, lifted the lid reverently. She sighed in admiration. It contained his elephant collection; small carved ebony and sandalwood elephants gleaming black and russet brown, multicoloured painted elephants some in full Perahera garb, and two miniscule ivory elephants. She was deeply impressed.

Johann was the same age as her and had always had a thing about elephants.

The last time they had seen each other their mothers had gone shopping in Colombo and had taken them to the zoo afterwards. They had gone for an elephant ride and then seen the elephants performing; circling around in a ring and supposedly doing a dance. Leila had liked the ride best. Johann had held her hand tightly and told her he would never let her fall. She had believed him. She smiled at him now and gestured towards the box. He nodded eagerly and his eyes gleamed with excitement and approval when she chose his favourite, a small sandalwood elephant. She placed it upright on her palm and stroked it gently.

"That's Diyon, he's going to be the ruler of the elephants one day. He's too small right now, but when he grows a little bigger he's going to challenge Ashan. He pointed to the largest of the little elephants that gleamed black and boasted pointy ivory tusks. Leila was about to argue that Diyon was never going to get any bigger, but then thought of all the fantastical adventures her cloth dolls had encountered that morning when she had played with Charlotte. These were Johann's dolls. She wouldn't spoil his game with them. The more she stared at them and saw how beautiful each was in its own way, the more she began to believe that Diyon might just grow big enough to challenge Ashan. She pulled Johann to a corner of the room furthest from the adults and they sat on the floor together removing the elephants one by one from the box and arranging them in a circle between them.

Sylvia, from her seat on the large couch at the centre of the room, looked with deep pleasure at her son and Leila playing together. "Don't you wish you still had a child's imagination?" She smiled at both Emma and Greta. Emma nodded in silent assent.

Greta's brow furrowed with annoyance. "Imagination is one thing, but there's a lot to be said for good manners. Leila, come and say hello to Aunty Sylvie please." Her voice conveyed annoyance, but had none of the harshness of the morning in it: something those outside the family must never see.

Leila stood obediently and hurried to Sylvia's side. "Oh, you didn't have to, beautiful girl, but let me kiss you while you're here!" Sylvia give her a big kiss and a hug and squeezed her cheek. "You get prettier every time I see you." She pushed Leila back towards Johann. She adored her little boy, but she had always wanted a daughter.

Leila liked Aunty Sylvie. She could certainly do without having her cheeks pinched and being told over and over again how pretty she was, especially as this seemed to annoy Mummy sometimes. But Aunty Sylvie genuinely liked her and always brought Johann along. Most times they saw her they went somewhere and had ice cream, or a walk in a park, or at the very least afternoon tea and cakes in one of their houses. What's more, there were times when her mother seemed to like her more because Aunty Sylvie liked her, or to see her differently or maybe even to be proud of her. A bit like the way she saw elephants through Johann's eyes when he was around. She ran back to him and they recommenced their play, a serious episode in the dramatic life of the boxed elephants.

Sylvia turned to Emma. "So, Cynthia seems to be coping well with the twins starting school, doesn't she? I'm not at all sure how I'll cope when Johann starts next year." She turned to include Greta. "What about you, Greta, do you think it's harder when they are only children? Maybe it would be a relief to have twins start school. I just can't imagine raising children without an ayah, let alone three boys and no servants at all!" She was turning from Greta to Emma and back again as she spoke, the words spilling out of her.

Emma shifted slightly in her seat. "I haven't heard from Cynthia for a few weeks, but of course that makes sense now. I just can't imagine how I lost track of the time. The twins would have started school a few weeks ago."

"Yes, just around the time of Leila's birthday. I remember chatting to Johann about it, and about them starting school, on our way here to the party. Of course, he wasn't at all interested, especially when I told him you were having a magician. He was so excited. Took days to stop talking about it!"

Emma looked perplexed. Such an important milestone in her grandsons' lives and a huge thing for Cynthia: her youngest children off to school. How had she forgotten?

Greta studied her mother with a bemused expression, her brow arched. It entertained her immensely to see her mother upset, caught short in her relating to Cynthia. She turned to Sylvia, intent on finding a way to hurt her mother, show her up further, if she could. "Sounds like you and Cynthie are as close as ever Sylvie, that she relies on you, confides in you. Do you write to each other often?"

Sylvia felt momentarily confused by the intensity in Greta's voice; it seemed strange, uncalled for. She had no understanding of guile. She spoke to Greta, trying her best to satisfy her, but quite at a loss to know what was wanted. "No, not that often. I'm not a great letter writer. But I ring her from time to time. She was my best friend all through school, I can't let that go. Just lucky I caught her when she needed to talk I guess." She beamed at Greta, hoping she could see how loyal she was to her sister and that this would please her. Greta fought to maintain a neutral expression. She had succeeded in nothing but stirring her own jealousy. Sylvia smiled broadly at Emma next.

Emma patted her hand. "Thank you. It sounds like you rang her at just the right time." She resolved to write to Cynthia as soon as she got home. She was not in a financial position to afford phone calls except in case of emergency, and neither was Cynthia anymore. They rarely spoke. She missed her older daughter's voice. She chose to dare Greta's rage: she needed to know. "How did she sound?"

"Oh, just the same. Maybe a little sad." Sylvia looked at Emma, and suddenly saw how much older she looked. She had been a constant visitor in this woman's home all through her childhood and teens. Emma's small house, her running her own business, Cynthia's mysterious and absent father, the fact of his sudden death, all these things had brought a sense of something that was very wrong and yet strangely exciting. Emma had always been there, and had been kind and welcoming. It was odd to suddenly see her as so much older and to glimpse the sadness in her. Of course, she must miss Cynthia terribly! They were so close. How had it never occurred to her until now? She tried her best to help. "Have you thought of going to visit? I'm sure she'd be so thrilled!"

Emma knew that it would take only a word from her and Cynthia and Ernest would find the money for her passage, somehow. But only if she were going to England to live with them. They had no money for holidays themselves, let alone a holiday visit for her. Sylvia Kelly had not the slightest idea about money; its value, the things it enabled or prevented, what it meant to work for it and to do without. She had always taken the things that ample money allowed for granted, could not see her blindness to the struggles of those without it. Emma liked her, despite this naivety or clumsiness. She doubted this state of affairs could persist for anyone of Burgher origin much longer. She wondered how Sylvia would cope. Her husband Frank had a sound head, perhaps they would manage. She smiled at Sylvia. "I think if I go I'll be going for good, and I'm not ready to leave Ceylon quite yet."

"Oh Lord, this perpetual conversation! Who's leaving next? How long can we stay? Is there any life here for the children? I'm so sick of it!"

Sylvia looked at Greta in surprise, and then became uncharacteristically serious. "I didn't know you'd been thinking about it at all, Greta. I certainly try my best not to, though I'm sure Frank's been hinting at it recently."

Greta lightened her tone immediately. "Sorry, Sylvie. Maybe it has to do with the party tonight. I'm sure there's something going on. It sounds like such a big do. The Leembruggens never throw parties without a reason." She glanced at her friend coyly. "Do you know what it's about?"

Sylvia giggled. "I'm sworn to secrecy!" She ran her hand across her lips. "Sheila wouldn't forgive me if I said a word."

Greta's curiosity and excitement intensified immediately. Sheila Leembruggen had been at the same school as her and was a couple of years younger. She smiled at Sylvia. "That's fine. I won't press the matter." Sylvia looked a little disappointed that she had given up so easily. But Greta didn't care. She felt a huge wave of relief. Something to do with Sheila had to be fun and more interesting than yet another farewell, or some great business achievement by Sheila's father, Lester. He was a friend of Jeff's. Jeff had many older friends and associates. At times, it seemed to exaggerate the ten-year age difference between them.

Thank heavens for Kingsley. He had been one of Jeff's closest friends since boyhood. He and Jeff worked together and he seemed to spend as much time in their home as his own. He had come on holiday with them on more than one occasion. He genuinely liked her, loved to play cards, to dance, to tell jokes; he made her feel that she and Jeff were perfect for each other. Greta smiled. "I'm sure Kingsley's coming tonight. Between he and Jeff I'll be able to spend the night dancing if nothing else."

"Yes, Kingsley's an amazing dancer. You'd think someone would have landed him for that alone. I don't understand how he's still single. Lawyers are so desirable as husbands. But Jeff took his time too, didn't he?"

"We've been married more than seven years."

Sylvia seemed not to notice the dryness and irritation in Greta's voice. She smiled at her in a conspiratorial way. "I've wondered sometimes if Kingsley's not just a little bit in love with you, Greta?"

Greta beamed. "Don't be ridiculous, Sylvie! He's Jeff's best friend!" But she was clearly pleased with the suggestion.

Sylvia suddenly blushed and turned to Emma. "I'm so sorry, Mrs de Zylva, I shouldn't talk about such things. I know you don't like gossip."

Emma smiled at her kindly. "I didn't hear any gossip, Sylvia, just a fantasy. But it's important to know the difference, isn't it? Friendships can be ruined for no good cause."

Greta was clasping the wooden arms of the chair in which she was seated. Her fingers had gone white at the knuckles. Were both women baiting her? No, Sylvia was too simple for that. Her rekindled rage focused, as ever, on her mother. She fought to keep her voice low, and even more to stop it from trembling. She must not let Sylvia see her rage at her mother, yet she could not fully silence herself. She struggled to keep her tone of voice as neutral as she could. "I can't remember you ever being my champion in the face of gossip."

Emma felt shocked anew by her daughter's selective memory and her lack of gratitude for all she had done to protect her from precisely this. Her voice was soft but clear. "You don't remember many things, Greta. But I wasn't thinking of you, I was thinking of myself and what I've had to contend with."

"You?" Greta could not bear it. Could her mother possibly believe that she deserved sympathy? After all she had done to ruin her life as a child, and the fact that in leaving her father she most likely caused his death? She stood abruptly and walked out of the room with no word to anyone.

Sylvia turned to Emma in concern. "Is Greta alright? I'm sorry if I've said anything out of turn, I was only making an observation." She giggled nervously. "Or as you say, discussing a fantasy." She suddenly remembered that Cynthia had been very angry with Greta about something in her teens. She had hinted that it might have been scandalous, but had stopped herself from saying anything more about it. Sylvia had noticed Greta's beauty even back then but being three years younger had made her seem quite irrelevant, especially as she and Cynthia were not close, and Cynthia had clearly never liked her sister.

Sylvia now considered Greta just as good a friend as Cynthia, perhaps more so, as Cynthia had left for England years ago and appeared to have no intention of returning for a holiday any time soon. Yet, she couldn't shake it, something to do with Greta had been hushed up, she was sure of it. But how could that matter now? Whatever had happened was ancient history. Jeff and Greta were the perfect couple.

For a moment, Emma doubted Sylvia could be quite as naive as she appeared: was there a crafted barb in this conversation? But she put the thought from her. She had known this young woman since she was a girl. She preferred to think she did not have such a thing in her, prevalent though it may be in those around her. Emma had become skilled through necessity at the art of ignoring slights and innuendo, in simply keeping on. "I'm sure she's just gone to check on her dress. The tailor's been here all morning and she's so excited about this party tonight."

"I suppose it must be a relief not to make Greta's clothes for her these days? Gives you more time to spend with her and with Leila?"

"It's Greta's choice, not mine. But yes, that may well be why."

Leila heard her name and looked up from her game and listened to the conversation. She had heard lots of times that her Gran made beautiful clothes for lots of other people. Mummy never talked about it. But Mummy and Daddy's friends sometimes did. So, the reason that Gran was so good at sewing, but never made any clothes for her or for Mummy, was that Mummy didn't want her to. It made sense at last. She looked back at Johann as he made two of his elephants charge at each other.

They all waited for Greta to return and soon her energetic step brought her back into the room. "I just went to check how cook was doing. Come on, everyone. Leila, Johann, pack up your toys and go wash your hands. Let's go through for lunch."

Emma did not look at her daughter. In the last few hours she had behaved more erratically than at any other time since the eve of her wedding, or perhaps during her pregnancies. Something was surely amiss, but she had no idea what. She had worked very hard to maintain a regular and stable relationship with Greta and had thought that she had succeeded. The fact that Jeff was deeply fond of her had certainly helped. The anxious, agitated, aggressive behaviour that Greta was displaying today raised deep fears in her.

Greta did not have her father's drinking problem, in fact, she abhorred alcohol. It made her sudden lack of stability even more frightening. It was not the drink that had her in its grip, so why was this happening? Yet, Emma had never fully believed this of Jürgen either, much as she had longed to. The nastiness was in him, alcohol simply facilitated its expression. Worse than that, it had provided him with some strange absolution in his own eyes and in the estimation of many others, who found him amusing and who had never felt the barb of his destructiveness turned pointedly their way.

Sylvia followed Greta's lead, and even took her arm as they walked through to the dining room; making an attempt at gaiety, with a broad smile at Emma and the children. She was eager to lighten the mood that had grown so strangely sombre between them all. Emma followed behind. She touched Leila gently on the shoulder and ushered her off in the right direction as they neared the dining room. Leila led Johann down a side corridor to the bathroom to wash their hands as Mummy had instructed. They immediately began the next game; turning the lovely white cake of soap over and over under the water until it became increasingly foamy and slippery, then passing it from one to the other to see who would drop it first. Leila stopped suddenly and dried her hands with care, passing the towel to Johann. He looked at her. "Your Mum's cross today, isn't she?"

Leila didn't reply, but she nodded suddenly and headed for the dining room, walking faster than usual and just a little ahead of him.

Greta sat at the head of the table with Sylvia on her right and Emma on her left. Leila quickly took the seat that was set next to her grandmother. Johann pulled a face as he climbed onto the chair next to his mother.

"What is it, darling? Do you want to sit next to Leila?" He nodded wordlessly and Sylvia turned to Greta. "You don't mind, do you? I'll just set him up over there and they can chat better." She was on her feet and moving his place mat, cutlery and glass to the opposite side of the table, next to Leila, before Greta could respond.

"Good thing it's a big table." Greta's tone was dry and tinged with annoyance. Sylvia, seemingly oblivious, bustled back to her chair and sat expectantly as Rani and Harold brought in the dishes of food. Everyone's mood lifted immediately as delicious aromas filled the room. "Rotis, Johann." Greta's dry tone persisted. She seemed on the verge of insulting her guests. Emma was considering how to intervene before Greta said anything more to cause offence.

But Johann looked directly at Greta. He was used to being adored and indulged and he knew that she liked him. "Thanks, Auntie, you always spoil me!" He grinned at her cheekily and she burst out laughing. The tension between all of them eased and they began to help themselves to the rotis, fish curry, sambal and chutneys. Johann looked to his mother this time. "Can we use fingers?"

But Greta responded before Sylvia could. "No, Johann, only the servants eat with their fingers in this house!"

Rani and Harold were leaving, but were still within earshot. Emma was deeply annoyed. Greta knew better. She had taught her better. Was this how she conducted her household in general, or was it a further indication of something unravelling in her today? It challenged Emma's conviction that Greta knew how to behave in company, that only she would be privy to her worst side.

Sylvia looked quite taken aback. She turned to Greta. "Lots of our friends eat with their fingers, Greta. There's an art to it. Johann has been practising."

It was the most assertive thing that Emma had ever heard this young woman say. It recognised both the class and racial slur that had been implied, as both Sinhalese and Tamils of the highest class ate with their fingers in polite society unless they chose to do otherwise. It was the British and the Burghers who adhered to European custom and cutlery, and most of the British had left the country.

Leila looked at her mother with a new kind of fear. Mummy was being horrible to everyone today, not just to her. It had started with the way she had talked to Charlotte. She had been rude to Gran lots of times in the past, but now she was being mean to Rani, Harold, Aunty Sylvie and even to Johann. She had never been cross with Johann before. She loved boys. One of Leila's theories about why her mother didn't like or love her was that her mother must have wanted a boy, that she was a big disappointment, especially as Aunty Cynthia had three boys including twins! How could one girl possibly make up for that? If she was being so mean now, how would she be when everyone left? She hoped that Gran would stay until Daddy got home as she usually did. Mummy was always better when Daddy was around. But maybe she would even be mean to him today? Nothing was certain.

Johann kicked her under the table. He was hungry and the food was delicious. He had decided not to pursue the matter and was handling his spoon and fork with great dexterity: an exemplary display to any adult who might mistakenly have thought his request meant he was not capable. He wanted Leila to eat too, so that they could leave the table long before the adults finished and have a chance to play in the garden. "Here, Leila, let me pass you this." He handed her a small dish of curry.

Greta smiled at him and turned to Sylvia. "He's a real little gentleman. Such manners at four!"

Sylvia laughed with pleasure while Emma worked to hide her distaste. So simple, to charm someone, make them forget your rudeness. Just like your father. She wished she could see her daughter differently, but right now it was impossible. Leila felt her mother's eyes on her as she took the dish from Johann. She must be careful, must not spill it. She wished they would all look away. She knew she was sure to drop it if they kept looking at her and then Mummy would get angry; in front of all these people, she'd say something awful. Her hand began to tremble. Someone took the dish from her and served some of the curry onto her plate. Soon there were two rotis there as well, and a spoonful of coconut sambal, which she loved.

"There you are, sweetheart." Emma turned to her daughter. "Can I pass anything to you, Greta?"

Greta's lip curled as she reached for a dish and her mother handed it to her, but she said nothing.

CHAPTER TWO

Nuwara Eliya and Colombo, February to April 1942

Emma sat at her dressing table by the large bay windows
of her bedroom and looked out at the lush vegetation, a
torrent of intense greenness that plummeted unexpectedly into a mist-shrouded valley, then re-emerged in a new and
quite different form on the hillsides covered in tea bushes far
into the distance. The coolness of the upcountry air seemed to
chill her bones. She could not remember when she had truly
felt warm. Surely in Colombo last Christmas, in the heat and
the bustle of the capital; its streets now invaded by jeeps and
British, Australian, and American sailors and army personnel.
But this coldness had been present even there. There was something wrong with her, really wrong. She was sure of it.

She had not been herself, had never really recovered after
haemorrhaging profusely at the time of Greta's birth, four
years ago. The doctors had said she was lucky to survive, giving birth here and not in Colombo. She remembered almost
nothing of the bumpy nightmare drive to Colombo two days
later, with Jürgen cursing most of the way. He had drunk
far too much scotch, but had insisted he was sober. He had
dropped her at the entrance to the hospital and left her there
with no word to anyone, and, she later found out, had nearly
skidded to his death on the windy upcountry dirt roads, in his
wild drive back to the plantation. She had been left to convey

her condition to a nursing sister, to demand to see a doctor urgently, not knowing if the words she strove for had actually been spoken or not. There had been fevered nights and days that followed, stretching endlessly. She found it hard to trace, in any form, something that might be counted a true memory of that time.

At some point during the course of her stay in hospital her cousin Inez had discovered she was there. She had rallied the family to visit, to make sure Emma had a regular supply of home-cooked food, to help her gain the strength she needed to return to her husband and daughters in the hill country. How hard it had been to accept this help, however much she knew it was essential to her, for with it came the family's implicit pity and disapproval that she had landed herself in this predicament. She had been the most beautiful of them all, the one feted for a great match. Instead she had chosen a renowned philanderer.

She had returned eventually to her home, to her daughters and her husband. There she had found that Cynthia, at three, had missed her terribly, had been inconsolable, had pined for her and feared her dead, while her newborn baby, Greta, was held closely in her ayah's arms. Emma found herself strangely grateful that the ayah, Anesha, could love this baby girl for whom she had no energy; a child conceived in hatred, not love, and born in a deluge of pain and blood that had almost killed her.

She sat at her dressing table and brushed her long curly hair, trying to tame it, then wound it into a tight bun at the nape of her neck. He had left early to see his foreman, to sort out some issue that was affecting either tea production or quality, she couldn't remember which. She could no longer feign interest. She had come to abhor the plantation life with its never-ending round of meaningless parties and gossiping cliques. At the heart of it she was tired of her loveless life, the contract she and

Jürgen shared, the pretence they called marriage. Perhaps it was just this that was draining the life and warmth from her.

* * *

"You'll see, Cynthie! I'm going to beat you for sure." Greta turned her head slightly and shouted over her shoulder as she ran up the driveway. She could hear the sound of tyres crunching on gravel.

"Don't be an idiot! You're half my size. You live in a dream world!" Cynthia jumped hurriedly from the lowest branch of the guava tree she had been perched in, but stumbled as she did so and fell to the ground.

"I'll tell Daddy you called me an idiot!" Greta ran for all she was worth, determined to reach their father first.

Cynthia got to her feet and the two little girls bolted through the bank of dense azaleas and rhododendrons and broke onto the semi-circle of lawn in front of their plantation bungalow just as their father's Bentley pulled to a halt by the porch. Greta jumped up onto the running board of her father's car. He opened the door gingerly and peered around at her standing just next to the rear passenger's door. He feigned complete surprise, then burst into laughter.

Greta laughed too; a triumphant gurgling laugh. "Oh Daddy, you didn't know it was me, did you? You thought it was Cynthie, but I beat her this time!"

Jürgen de Zylva scooped his four-year-old daughter into his arms and tossed her into the air, catching her just as her older sister slammed into him from the side. "Cynthia! I could have dropped your sister!"

"But you never would, Dad, you're much too strong!"

He hoisted both giggling girls up, one on each shoulder, and held on firmly to their legs as he made his way towards the house. He was six foot four inches tall and his shoulders were correspondingly broad, suitably safe for a shoulder-ride. He lowered them to the ground and opened the front door. His tone of voice changed to something very different as he called out loudly. "Emma! Emma!" He stopped shouting and mumbled discontentedly to his daughters. "It would be wonderful if I got even a skerrick of enthusiasm from your mother for a change."

Cynthia's face clouded immediately and she hurried away to find their mother, to let her know that their father must have been drinking, because it was only if he had been drinking that he would shout in this way. But Greta seemed not to understand any of this. She reached for her father's hand and clung to it. "Come on, Daddy, don't be grumpy. I've been waiting all day to see you. Come, let's go play a game."

Jürgen looked down at his little daughter, and his bloodshot eyes filled with tears of sentimentality. "Have you, Baby Girl? You've been waiting for me! Well that's a fine thing indeed, isn't it? It's what any man would live or die for. To be missed by his own daughter, by the people he loves."

He heard a soft swishing sound and looked up to see his daughters' ayah standing in the doorway to the dining room, gazing at him with deep pleasure and smiling a knowing smile. She swayed her hips as she stood and her beautiful silk sari made again the soft swishing sound that had caught his attention. Her gazed at her in surprise, then sudden fear. "Anesha, are you crazy? What are you doing wearing that here? It was a gift for a special time, another place."

The young woman walked towards him filled with feminine grace, making her bid to lay claim to him, seeming not to see the little girl clinging to his hand and staring in bewilderment at the ayah she loved who was behaving so strangely. Anesha stood directly in front of him. "You do not like me in it, Jürgen?"

He let go of his daughter's hand and his arm encircled the beautiful, slender waist before him as he pulled Anesha's body hard against his. "I love you in it!" He kissed her passionately on the lips.

"Really, Jürgen? In the hallway of our home? With Greta there, beside you?" Emma was pale, with the pallor of long-term ill health, but all frailty had left her. Her voice was calm and soft, but carried in it the steel of a determination he had never guessed she possessed. She looked him directly in the eyes, then did the same to Anesha. The younger woman stared at her with triumph at first but could not sustain the steady gaze that confronted her. She lowered her eyes. Her mistress had always treated her with kindness; she could not forget this completely, however compelling and exciting she found her master.

Emma turned back to her husband. "Please take your woman and leave. I'll be gone as soon as I can, and you can have the house back. It will take me a few days to make arrangements, to pack all of the girls' things and those things that are mine."

He looked at her in disbelief. "Where will you go?"

"To Colombo of course."

"You think you can manage without me? You've barely been well enough to do the most basic entertaining since Greta's birth, to be any kind of a wife at all, and you're going to make your own way in Colombo?"

"Yes, that's exactly what I'm going to do."

"Do this, humiliate me in this way, and I will not take you back. You understand me?" His voice was filled with viciousness. Intimidation had always succeeded. He was sure it would again.

"I understand you completely. Please leave and take your woman. I don't care what either of you do once I'm gone." Emma stepped closer and Anesha gasped and moved quickly to one side, out of reach. But Emma reached forward and took her little daughter's hand and pulled her away.

Greta began to sob. "I don't want Daddy to go. I want him to come with us. I want to stay with Daddy!" She started to cry as Emma lifted her into her arms. She wriggled and tried to get down.

Cynthia, who had been listening from the next room, ran to her mother's side and shouted at Greta. "Stop it! Stop being such a baby. Can't you see he's with her. He doesn't want any of us!" She glared at her father and her ayah with hatred.

"Alright! Have it your way! But don't expect to hear from me again, any of you!" Jürgen looked pointedly at Emma, but then strangely at both of his daughters as well.

Cynthia glared back at him, but Greta began to cry and scream. "No, Daddy, no! Don't go!"

He took Anesha by the hand and pulled her with him. She had lost the edge of excitement that had driven her to make this play, to reveal the reality of a situation that she was tired of in its current form. She did not know fully what she had expected. But she saw now it was not this. She glanced briefly at the little girls she had cared for since they were babies. She could not look at her mistress again. The secret gloating that she had cherished for so long had completely dissipated. If he could leave not just his wife but his daughters too so easily, what would become of her?

* * *

The girls were finally asleep and Emma sat on her bed. The bedside lamp glowed, its light soft and warm. It felt strangely cheery to her. How could that be? Greta had cried and screamed and had hit out at her and even at Cynthia repeatedly, until Emma had to restrain the little girl physically, to shut her in her room, where at last she had cried herself to sleep, inconsolable. It was terrible, just terrible. She looked at Cynthia fast asleep in the bed beside her, unwilling to return to the room she shared with her sister. What a horrible mess she had made of it all. Yet, she felt happier, freer than she had felt for so many years.

She could not understand it. She was more alone in the world than at any time since her own mother died when she was fourteen, giving birth to her little sister, who she never saw. They were buried together. Her father had not let her attend the funeral, would not speak her mother's name. He had taken away all photographs of her, except the one she kept in her dresser hidden from him. He had retreated into his work and had spent his nights at his club, or so she had believed. It was only after his death, when she was in her early twenties, that she discovered how else he passed his time, for he had gambled away most of their wealth.

She realised at last and with a strange clarity that she had married Jürgen all those years ago to flee the shame, to flee Colombo. But had instead found herself in a more arid place than any she might have imagined. So, it did make sense. Of course, leaving the emotional desolation of their relationship would cheer her. Whatever she had to do to survive without him, she would do it.

She remembered suddenly that she had grown up in a world of servants and thought at once of her ayah, who had stayed on as a house servant, who had always offered her kindness and love. She had not been alone then, and she was not alone now. She had these two little girls of her own to care for and to raise. She had a chance to live her life her way, without Jürgen. She smiled as she stroked Cynthia's hair. Her older daughter loved her so fiercely; the absolute knowledge and truth of this gave her the strength to do whatever was needed. Her daughters must have a better life. She rationally included Greta, although emotionally she often struggled with a sense of revulsion whenever her tiny daughter reminded her too forcibly of the father she so resembled.

She tried to plan her next move. In the morning, she would telephone her cousin Inez, the daughter of her mother's brother, her only uncle, who had died years ago of malaria. All their childhood Inez had been jealous of her for having a father to care for her, envious of both her wealth and her beauty. Their circumstances were completely reversed now. Inez had married well. Her husband Edward was both wealthy and educated. She had risen in Burgher society, even as Emma had lost any status she once had, or so she believed.

Yet, if this was another chance for Inez to rescue her, to feel superior, it didn't matter. Nothing mattered but to get away safely, with everything she wanted to take with her. She knew there would be no coming back, no asking for anything left behind. Jürgen even now would not fully believe that she could leave him. Her move to Colombo had to be organised swiftly, before he returned in some drunken rage and saw its reality. Anything was possible if that were to happen. She had seen it in his eyes; he could not bear to know that he had lost his power over her. She knew him well enough to realise that he was capable of losing his sense of control completely with her, and maybe now with the girls too. They had to go.

* * *

Greta sat beside Cynthia as the car pulled to a halt. She felt exhausted and nauseated after the hours of driving down windy roads in the back of the car, squashed in tight in the middle of the back seat with pillows and bedding piled in beside her. Cynthia could see out of the window, but she was too short to see anything. She wanted Anesha. She wanted her father. She couldn't remember a single morning that Anesha had not kissed her good morning, or helped her get dressed, or brushed her hair and told her how beautiful she was and that she would always be her own very special little girl. Sometimes she might not see her father for days, but she knew he felt the same way about her, exactly the same way. But they were both gone, and she was going somewhere far away, where they might never find her. She was going with her mother and with Cynthia, and Cynthia was her mother's very special girl.

She had always been sure about that too. She could play with Cynthia at times, but she could see that Cynthia had never truly liked her. They were sisters, that was all.

The car door opened and her mother helped Cynthia out, then reached in to take her hand. She wanted to scream and make a fuss, as big a noise as she could make, to show them both how angry she was. But she was also very frightened that her mother would just shut her away in a room again, in a strange room this time. Maybe she would leave her with strange people if she didn't behave. She realised suddenly that she needed to go to the toilet. She didn't want to ask, but she'd have to, otherwise she might wet her jungies and Cynthia would call her a baby again. There was a woman she didn't know standing outside the car next to her mother. She sidled along the seat and whispered in her mother's ear as she bent to help her out of the car.

"Of course, Greta, come along. It will be alright. I promise." Her mother spoke to the woman beside her softly, too softly for her to hear. The woman laughed and said something back. She felt so ashamed that the first thing this stranger should know about her was that she had to rush to the toilet. She didn't look up as she hurried along beside her mother trying her best to hide herself in the folds of her mother's full skirt. Her mother led her along the side of a big house and through a door into a dark hallway and then to a toilet. There was a strange hole in the floor, not a proper toilet. Her mother pulled a face. "I'm sorry, Greta, you'll just have to put your feet on either side like this and squat." Her mother held up her own skirt and showed her how to do it, then lifted up her dress and pulled down her jungies. Her mother held them while she squatted over the hole in the floor.

She couldn't do anything. It just wouldn't come out. She always went to the toilet by herself. She was being treated like a baby. She wanted to go home. She wanted Anesha. She began to cry, long hard sobs of pain.

"Greta, I'm sorry. I really am. I know this is very hard. That lady is my cousin Inez. We'll be staying with her for a little while. As short a time as I can possibly manage. But we have to stay here right now. And you need to go to the toilet if you can."

Her mother's voice wasn't angry but it was very tense. She could tell she was being a nuisance.

"Do you want me to wait outside? Will that be better?"

"No! No!" She hadn't meant to scream, she just had. She was terrified of the small dark smelly room, terrified she might fall down the hole in the ground.

"Stop screaming, Greta! I won't go anywhere. Just see if you can do anything or we'll have to leave."

"She's such a baby, Mum! They have toilets like that at our school in Nuwara Eliya!" Cynthia had followed at a distance and opened the toilet door a crack. She was peering in.

"Cynthia, you're not helping! Greta has never had to use a toilet like this before. Go back to the others. We'll come soon." Emma's voice was uncharacteristically stern and Cynthia hurried away.

Somehow, Greta went to the toilet in the end. She felt hot and flustered as she walked back up the path and into the house through another door. She imagined that Cynthia and the lady would probably be laughing at her. Instead she found them sitting on sofas and drinking cold drinks, or at least the dark lady who looked at her intensely was doing that. Cynthia was kneeling at a low table and eating little sandwiches from a china plate in the centre of the table.

"She's the image of Jürgen, isn't she?"

The lady was talking to her mother. Was she talking about her father? His name was Jürgen. Was she talking about her?

"Have some sandwiches, Greta."

Her mother was talking to her. She knelt on the floor next to Cynthia and reached for a sandwich. She felt sick. She held on to the sandwich. She took a bite and tried to swallow.

* * *

The annex was small, but definitely sufficient for their needs. It had two bedrooms, a little lounge and kitchen and a proper Western bathroom and toilet. Edward was insistent that Emma and the girls could stay as long as was needed. Many houses in Colombo's wealthier suburbs had been commandeered by the British military. He felt fortunate to have retained his home. Other relatives, evicted from their homes in such a way, or in need and poorer circumstances than he, had availed themselves of his generosity before. His offer was completely genuine, and heartfelt. If her relationship with Inez were different Emma might have thought this a refuge, where she could take her time to find the right way forward. As things were, she knew she had to find the means to earn a living and achieve self-sufficiency quickly. Inez was being increasingly strange with her daughters. She had not left Jürgen for this.

* * *

They all told her to work for the British. It was a time like no other. The world was at war, and the major impact in Ceylon to date was the sudden presence of thousands of military personnel in the island. This had changed things in Burgher society quite drastically, as there was a sudden need for young women with a good knowledge of English in these military units. Burgher girls fitted the requirements exactly and were being employed en masse, much to the chagrin of their fathers and brothers. It gave these young women new-found financial freedom and access to men and ways of relating that they had only seen in the movies.

Emma had done a course in shorthand and typing shortly before she married Jürgen, when she had thought she might need to support herself financially. She was very fast at both, had topped her class. But she had never worked and she hated the thought of working for the British. She had no time for them. She'd had virtually no contact with them until she moved to the hill country after marrying Jürgen. Colombo society was divided into its own defined circles. She had mixed almost exclusively with other Burghers or with middle- and upper-middle-class Sinhalese and Tamil girls who were also Christians and who attended the same private school as she did.

Her people, the Burghers, were the descendants of the Europeans who had stayed in Ceylon after successive waves of colonisation, those who could not leave the beautiful island they had come to exploit. Sometimes intermarrying with Sinhalese or Tamil Christians, as a group they identified most with their European heritage and considered themselves European.

In the hill country, living in close proximity to the British in a tiny community, she struggled with a different form of prejudice; for it was suddenly obvious to her that many of the British did not see the Burghers the way they saw themselves. She met some British families who were friendly and open, but in the main found herself excluded by a sense of superiority, privilege and private clubs. In Colombo, she had been insulated from the reality that this was exactly how most Burghers behaved to the majority of Sinhalese and Tamils. She had never realised that most of the British in Ceylon might look down on her because she was a Burgher and therefore Eurasian.

As a newly married woman in the hill country she had found herself detesting the British planters that she met, who lacked all sophistication, who would work alongside Jürgen as a fellow planter, yet seemed to deem it an honour should they treat him as an equal at all. He had never been affected by it, had held his own in any company, with anyone. His father had gone to Oxford and he knew that, had circumstances been different, he would have gone there as well. She was the one who had become increasingly isolated. She had felt certain that all the British women she met were of the worst sort. She had ignored any overtures from fellow Burgher women who were planters' wives and had declined most invitations that came her way, until she had no longer been included on anyone's list. She had avoided the tennis club where both groups of women mixed and where it seemed that destroying reputations was the source of greatest interest and pleasure.

She now recognised that it might have been her own shame at being with someone like Jürgen that had limited her most, for she had no desire to see pity in any woman's eyes, be they British or Burgher. Of course, she could work for the British, or the Americans, or any military organisation that would have her. They paid well from what she had heard. The thing was possible, for a time, especially if there were hope of something more.

An idea had come to her late one night, while the girls were sleeping. She had remembered her teens spent in her family home, a large house just a few streets from this one, and her passion for designing clothes. She had found wonderful European designs and modified them. Later she had sketched her own original creations and the gifted seamstress Martha Ferdinands would bring them to life once they decided on texture and fabric together. She would contact Martha and become her apprentice if she could, learn her art. She felt energised.

* * *

She stood and waited in front of the house. Colombo was so much hotter than the hill country, but comfortably so at this time in the morning. Even the oppressive humidity of the afternoon suited her better than the upcountry coolness. She was standing beneath the shade of one of the large flamboyant trees that spread their arms in an interlacing canopy of green leaves and bright orange-red blooms along the lovely residential road. A large army truck pulled in at the curb just behind her. The driver got down and unlatched the tailgate, then held his hand to help her climb up. "Sorry I'm late, Emma. Make sure

39

to tell the brass it was me that caused the problem won't you!" He laughed good naturedly as he pulled the tailgate back into place and latched it securely. Tommy, he was so friendly and playful. His deep tan accentuated the blueness of his eyes.

"There's no point flirting with Emma, she's married with two little girls!" Sixteen-year-old Deidre de Saram adjusted her dress and Tommy got a good look at her long golden-brown legs. All the young women in the back of the truck burst out laughing. Most of them were in their late teens or early twenties. He must have said something similar to each of them as he picked them up on his run this morning. It was a given, not one of them would mention a word against him, and he knew it. He flirted with them all. It was rumoured he had a girlfriend in Dehiwela. These British soldiers were completely different to the planters Emma had known. Friendly, open, and eager to be pleasant and kind, as they waited far from home for the anticipated and dreaded transfer to a combat arena. They knew it might come at any time; the next stage in this war, the one they might not survive.

The streets of Colombo were teeming with men in uniform: Australians, British, Americans. Some of the girls were frightened of them. They drove too fast and seemed too bold, especially the Australians with their more laconic way of talking and casual approach to manners. Others were excited by them. Emma, in one of her rare political conversations with Edward, discovered that there were dangerous elements among the Singhalese: those who hoped the Japanese would liberate them from British rule, who wished all these allies defeated.

The truck trundled on, past the racecourse that had been turned into an airfield by the British, along Reid Avenue and Thurston Road, where planes were neatly tucked in beneath the overarching boughs of the giant trees that lined these thoroughfares, so that they might not be seen from the air. The girls beside her were playing a game, who would be the first to spot a pilot near his plane. These girls and women who worked with her felt decades younger than her, if not in years, then in experience. In the main they were lately out of school and eager to see what life had in store. They also had a very different opportunity than their mothers and aunts had ever had, being provided with this ability and freedom to work.

Their fathers could not deny them this, they were helping the war effort and were needed. They were also courted and in high demand among the thousands of young men far from home. For them there was new-found, unexpected agency and the advent of war seemed more like a party. They were strangely carefree, unable to see that any danger might reach Ceylon, despite their daily drive past these planes in hiding from a threatened Japanese attack and even though it was well known that a large part of the British fleet was anchored in Trincomalee harbour, in the north of the island.

Emma was working three days a week, typing and copying coded letters into log books, sorting and filing papers. It was tedious work in one way, but well paid and strangely pleasant in another; for she genuinely enjoyed the company of the girls around her, while having almost nothing in common with them. She realised that she had never been like them. Her mother's death had robbed her of a stage of life they seemed to share; one of gaiety and camaraderie, even while the world was at war.

She had not heard from Jürgen in the three weeks since she had left him. She had begun to relax a little. It seemed he might let them go. It was all she could hope for. Any contact from her might make him take an interest again. Cynthia had begun school at Milagiriya. Emma assured herself she would repay Edward somehow for the year's tuition he had paid in advance. Did Inez know? She must. What was behind this generosity? Greta was being looked after by a house servant who she seemed to shadow all day. It was far from ideal, but Emma needed to work in order to save money, in order to leave.

On the days she wasn't working for the British military she spent as much time as possible with Martha Ferdinands,

41

working with her and learning all she could. She had not lost her knack, and was drafting her own patterns already. It was difficult to get materials, but Martha felt there would easily be work enough for two if they could really get going. The Americans seemed able to get hold of almost anything, and were keen to do so to win the favour of the local women. Martha had suggested that she and her girls move in. But it was too soon for another change. She needed to be certain.

On Sundays she longed to stop, stay in the house or spend time with her daughters in the local park. But first she must do what was required by her hosts. Together they attended the Dutch Reformed Church at Wolvendaal, now as a large extended family, no longer the childless couple, but rather a couple and the family members they were treating with both charity and concern. Cynthia and Greta went to Sunday school. Emma did her best to hold her head high, to listen to the sermon, to sing the hymns, and to smile at former acquaintances.

She had long given up the habit of church attendance. It belonged to the era when her mother was alive and when her life had been ordered and measured and safe; a time of wider social circles, of other friendly adults and children who came to play. It had been a time when school and friendships had been the greatest thing she had to contend with. The memory of it had a dreamlike quality, until her mother's face began to seep into her consciousness and her chest and neck constricted with pain. It happened this Sunday as she sang a hymn and realised it was one that her mother had loved.

After the service, Emma stood beside Inez and Edward in front of the church. People thronged around them, talking earnestly, laughing, gossiping. Her daughters came out from the building alongside the main church and ran to her. Cynthia took her hand and Greta stood by her side. Inez put her hand on the little girl's shoulder and held her firmly. Greta didn't like the feel of her fingers. They were bony and they held her tight. Did Aunty Inez think she was going to run away, or do something bad? She wished more than anything that she could do exactly that. This was the best time of the week for her, being out of that big house where no one laughed or played or had any fun, being in the world and seeing other people, knowing that maybe someone at this church or somewhere in the rest of Colombo might know her father or help her get some word to him about where she was. There was a chance she might be rescued.

"Emma Speldewinde? I thought it was you. It must be ten years!"

Emma looked at the man who had come up to them so eagerly. His face was open and excited, he seemed no older than his early thirties but his dark brown hair was already receding. Could this be Mervin Brohier? He had pursued her in her late teens, been one of a number of young men who had taken her to dances and parties. She had always assumed that his departure overseas was directly linked to his realisation that she wasn't interested in anything other than friendship with him. He was from a time before her father died, a time before Jürgen. "Mervin, it's good to see you." It was the truth, he had always been kind.

"Yes, and forgive me, Mrs de Zylva!" He glanced at her two little girls, then looked around. "Is your husband with you? I must introduce you to my wife. I have three sons you know."

"He's not here, Mervin." She looked at him plainly. "I left him. I'm staying with Inez and Edward." She got no further. He glanced briefly at her hosts and gave the briefest nod of recognition in their direction, then rushed away without any further word to her. She stared after him. "How extremely odd. I thought he was such a nice person."

Inez gave a short laugh. "I don't know how you're going to survive in Colombo! You've got no idea."

"There's the car. Shall we?" Edward seemed not to have heard or taken any interest in what had just happened. Emma was uncertain if he was truly oblivious to the world around

43

him and caught up in some preoccupation with his business concerns, or if he feigned ignorance so as not to have to deal with society's demands and his wife's poor behaviour. She suspected the latter. Perhaps because it had been her way of coping for so long. She knew it would no longer serve her. She had fled Colombo for the hill country and found a life of isolation and quiet desperation with Jürgen. She saw now that she would need to contend with people, keep attuned to their behaviour and make more sense of them, if she were to make any life for herself and her girls.

Greta climbed into the back of the car with her mother and sister. Aunty Inez sat in the front next to Uncle Edward who was driving. She began to think about the man who came up to Mummy and had rushed away as soon as he heard what Mummy said about leaving Daddy. He must think she had done something wrong. He certainly acted that way. Maybe he could get a message to Daddy, if she could talk to him at church. She realised she had no idea what he looked like. He said he had three sons. Could she ask for the man with three sons? Who could she ask? What was she going to do? She felt so hot and distressed, so angry with everyone, including herself. She began to sob quietly.

Emma put her arm around her daughter. "What is it Greta? What's wrong?"

"I want to go home."

Emma's back straightened. She patted her daughter's head and removed her arm. "We'll talk about this later, Greta. I will need to find us a home in Colombo." She was acutely aware of Inez sitting in the seat just in front of them.

"You know, Emma, that might be very difficult for you. Especially as you'll need someone to look after Greta while you're at work. If you do find somewhere to rent you can always leave her with us, at least until she's ready for school. I know you time your work around Cynthia's school hours.

44

We might consider paying both the girls' school tuition, if Greta stays on with us."

Emma said nothing. What she hated most of all was how tempted she was by the offer. It was very true, she had no idea what she could do with Greta. If she moved in with Martha Ferdinands and started dressmaking in earnest it would be very difficult to cope with Greta at the same time. If she were a more placid or cooperative child it would be completely different. But, as it was, she would have to be watched carefully, at all times. Emma sensed her daughter's deep distress and desire to run. It was so familiar to her from her own life with Jürgen; her sense of being trapped, her longing to escape him. Her daughter on the other hand was experiencing this in being with her, and wanted more than anything to be with her father. Emma had briefly considered this, letting him have Greta, but she feared he would hurt Greta in some way, just to punish her. It never occurred to her that she might be holding on to Greta in order to punish him.

* * *

It was early Easter morning and Cynthia and Greta were playing in the driveway in front of the annex. They had crept out quietly so as not to wake Mummy, as Cynthia said she was always so tired and needed more sleep. They had painted boiled eggs with her the afternoon before and put them in a beautiful coloured paper basket they had made. It was sitting on the table in the main house where Aunty Inez and Uncle Edward lived. They would get dressed in their best dresses and go to church when it was time for Mummy to get up. But they would also have a special lunch because it was Easter. Mummy had promised they could have ice cream.

There was a strip of garden to one side of the driveway and a low curved coconut tree that ran parallel to the ground for a short distance. Cynthia climbed it easily and sat a little way along it. Greta pulled herself onto the lowest flattest part of the trunk where she could balance easily then edged her way along the trunk until she was sitting beside her sister. Cynthia seemed in a good mood.

"School here is great fun you know. There are so many different children to play with, boys and girls. It's very different from the school I went to in Nuwara Eliya of course. When I got there! Dad would only drop me sometimes!"

Greta's whole body tensed at mention of their father. Cynthia hardly ever talked about him and her mother never did.

"I think if you come to Milagiriya next year you'll see what I mean. It can be fun to play!" Cynthia was being unusually generous. She was often very annoyed with Greta, who had never mixed with other children and had spent all her time with Anesha, their parents or with her. Greta didn't seem to know how to play with boys and girls her own age at all. She always sat next to her at Sunday school and never spoke to anyone. She was a real nuisance.

There was a loud noise above them, engines whirring through the sky above. Cynthia jumped down and Greta quickly made her way along the tree to a point where she could turn and lower herself down. She ran to join Cynthia who was staring up at a sky filled with planes. "Quick, see how many you can count before they're all gone!" Cynthia was excited and happy and Greta felt happy for a moment too. "Run inside and get Mum, she'll want to see this!" Greta hesitated. "Go on. I'll keep counting!"

Greta headed for the annex, she could just reach the handle of the back door to open it. She ran inside as Emma opened the door of her bedroom and came out in her dressing gown. Greta reached for her hand. "Mummy come, Cynthia says you have to come. There are so many planes. Is it for Easter?"

Emma grasped Greta's hand without answering. There was a loud booming sound outside followed by another and another. Emma began to run, gripping her younger daughter's hand.

"Cynthia, quickly! Come with me! Now!"

Cynthia turned to see in her mother's face the fear that she had heard in her voice. She didn't understand.

"Quickly, now!" Emma ran with Greta beside her, holding her hand tightly. Cynthia followed close behind. They reached the back of the main house and ran along the other side of it, to where a makeshift bomb shelter had been constructed in the cellar. The door was open, and Edward and two servants were squatting behind a pile of sandbags. Inez was crouching under a table in the middle of the small room. It was a dusty room with empty wine racks down one side, a former owner's folly in the tropics.

"Emma, girls over here!" Edward pointed at the large pile of sandbags, then ran to the door and slammed it shut. Immediately the room was in complete darkness. Someone whimpered. Edward groped his way slowly back and searched around on the top of the table until he found the torch he had placed there. He switched it on. "Silly of me, I should have taken this with me." He looked at the solemn faces around him, bewildered, or asking for surety in the strange yellow light. "It must be the Japanese. Just like Pearl Harbor, at a weekend. But why Easter Sunday? ..." His question had a plaintive ring to it.

* * *

"You know that a Japanese plane was shot down near Saint Thomas' College ... and another on the Galle Face Green!", "It's just a blessing that the Eastern Fleet weren't in the harbour", "... his sister died when that bomb fell on Mulleriyawa Mental Hospital ...", "... they had a radio warning and just ignored it you know ...", "... thank heavens for those Royal Air Force fighter planes at the racecourse, if they hadn't got

47

into the air …", "… but it's nothing compared to what happened at Trinco … so many died there …"

Emma walked among the throng heading into the church. It was the Sunday that followed the terrible events of Easter Sunday. Only a week had passed but their world had changed. Instead of the occasional greeting and quiet asides that were usual prior to a service the whole congregation was buzzing with the extraordinary and terrifying events of the previous week. Trincomalee had been bombed four days after Colombo, hundreds had died there, but the Japanese had not found the British Eastern Fleet, which together with some Royal Netherlands Navy warships had sailed to Addu Atoll in the Maldives. Any planned Japanese troop landing was evaded. The island and its people were safe for the moment, if stunned by the unthinkable; for the war had reached them in a whole new way.

The minister's voice was soothing; his message one of condolence for lives lost and also one of hope. Singapore had fallen to the Japanese only two months earlier, yet they had been saved from an invasion. Emma sat in the coolness of the aged building with its dense stone walls and high ceiling. She lost her connection to the people around her as she listened to the tone of the minister's voice, no longer discerning the words being said. Coming to Colombo had placed her life and her daughters' lives at risk. Many families were packing up and heading out of the capital. In the event of a Japanese invasion the hill country would undoubtedly be a safer place. Yet she knew she could never return. She felt a surge of nausea at the thought, not just of being close to Jürgen, but also of returning to the stultifying society that she abhorred. She lifted her head in silent defiance of anything in her that might contemplate this move. Such wasted years. It would not happen again.

Inez had been behaving even more strangely since the air raid. Simple pleasantries and greetings went ignored. She had walked away from the breakfast table that morning the moment Emma and the girls arrived and had not said a word in the car during the drive to church. Even Edward seemed uncomfortable with her current curtness. It was impossible to make any clear sense of her behaviour, but from something one of the servants said in passing it seemed possible that she was ashamed of having hidden under the table in the cellar while everyone else huddled next to sand bags. Emma had thought nothing of it. They were all frightened and she didn't know if the so-called bomb shelter would have offered any actual protection had the house been bombed.

After the service, Emma did not file out behind Inez and Edward. She had seen Martha Ferdinands some distance in front of her during the service and waited for her in the back vestibule of the church. She touched Martha's arm as she drew near and pulled her to a quiet corner. "Did you mean it, Martha? Can the girls and I come and stay? I know you'll be cramped."

"It's no problem at all, as long as you don't mind sharing a room together. There are two beds in my spare room already and I'm sure we can fit a camp bed in for Greta. She's such a little cutie."

"She's my main worry. I don't know how we'll get anything done and I'll still have to work for the military a couple of days a week, until I can build up a clientele. I finish by two and can pick Cynthia up after school on my way back to your place. But I can't ask you to look after Greta while I do all that?"

"Didn't Inez offer to look after her until she starts school next year?"

Emma winced. Martha must know she wanted to leave Inez and Edward's house because she was uncomfortable there, yet she was not taking up her thinly veiled request for help with Greta. What option did she have?

* * *

The lunch was served in silence. The food was on the table and the cook and house servant had both left. Cynthia and Greta looked to their mother to see if she would start to fill their plates. Mealtime with Uncle Edward and Aunty Inez was always uncomfortable. Edward smiled and offered a dish to Emma. She began to spoon rice onto each of the girl's plates and then onto her own.

"Really Edward? She comes first?"

Edward blanched. "Inez, Emma and her daughters are our guests." His voice was calm, his words distinct. He had feared an outburst for the last week. He knew that Inez had not coped well with the Japanese raid and the air battle last week, even though no one close to them had died or been injured.

Emma could sense the tension between the two of them. "I'm planning to move in with Martha Ferdinands next week."

Edward lifted his serviette from his lap and placed it on the table beside his plate. He was contemplating his next sentence.

"I've been thinking about this for some time, Edward. I'm eternally grateful to you both." She turned and looked at Inez as well, including her in the conversation, although Inez continued to stare directly ahead at the wall behind Emma and would not meet anyone's gaze. "In fact, Inez and I have talked about it on several occasions."

Edward lifted his right eyebrow in surprise and glanced towards his wife before returning his attention to Emma. "You can take whatever time you need, Emma."

"Thank you, Edward. I believe I have done exactly that." She looked at him intently. "Inez has offered that the two of you will look after Greta for me until I can stop working for the military and support myself with dressmaking. I hope that will be alright?"

"Of course, of course, and I am very happy to pay for the girls' education until you can afford it. I want you to know that."

50

"Thank you. I'm very grateful."

Greta climbed off her chair and ran into the adjoining room. She sank to the ground in the furthest corner of the room and hugged her knees. She began to sob and shake.

* * *

"Why this amazing generosity, Edward? Can we afford to support all our relatives in this way?"

"They're your family, Inez. We've talked about helping Emma out with the girls' school fees. I thought you'd be pleased."

"Did you? Really? You've offered her their entire schooling if need be, with no conditions!"

"What conditions were you thinking of exactly?"

"I thought we could get her to give us Greta. We might even adopt her."

"You'd take advantage of her misfortune to that degree?" He eyed his wife with sudden distaste and she saw it. He went on. "I knew Jürgen when we were boys. If his older brother hadn't died, if his parents had coped better, he might be a very different man. For that matter if Emma's mother hadn't died …"

"My father died and I coped."

Edward remained silent. He wondered how she would have fared had he not married her. She was a far more troubled person that he had ever suspected, and had a difficult side that was all too evident with Emma and her daughters in the house. It might be a real relief if they were to move out.

Inez stared at her husband, seeing him lost in thought. What was he thinking? Did he realise that she feared he had some age-old yearning or affection for her cousin? He gave not the slightest hint of it. It could be her jealously of Emma, that had plagued her all her life, returning to poison her mind and her marriage. She dared not talk of it. He might call her mad, lose his respect for her if she even hinted at such a thing. Would she

51

wound him? At times, she saw that her trust in him was in some way vital to him, gave him a sense of belief in himself, a strength to go on, even after the enduring disappointment they both faced in being childless.

CHAPTER THREE

Colombo, Friday 25th September 1964

"So? It sounds genuinely promising, don't you think?" Jeff van Buuren looked intently at his best friend and partner in his legal practice. He knew he was asking a lot of him. The heat of midday made the air around them oppressive, heightened the musky smell of teak and ebony that emanated from the wooden panels and furniture of the room and mixed with the rich smell of leather upholstery. The windows were open but half shaded by blinds pulled low. The room was in semi-darkness, illuminated only by the pale, yellow glow of the ceiling light in its bell-shaped antique glass shade, a relic of the colonial days they clung to. "Ronald would never be so optimistic unless he was sure he could deliver. Simply not in his make-up."

Kingsley stared at him. Jeff was tall, lean and strikingly handsome in the way some Burgher men are. The mix of Dutch, Portuguese, French and Scottish ancestry that was his Western heritage had combined with Sinhalese or Tamil blood from some generations back, obscured now and scarcely admitted, with a result that was compelling. Moreover, he took his physical presence and natural poise and charm for granted. In Ceylon or during his time studying or travelling abroad he had never known a world in which they did not exert their influence. Kingsley had been his friend from the time they had met as little boys at primary school at St Paul's Milagiriya. He had been in love with Jeff since the age of thirteen.

"Why Australia? Why not the States, Canada, Britain? You could settle near London. Greta would have her sister in Kent and Amy would be hundreds of miles to the north." Kingsley's sarcasm was palpable, though he baulked inwardly at his own insensitivity in mentioning Amy. He knew very well the part he had played in the end of Jeff's relationship with her, though Jeff may not understand, would never have suspected his motives. His jealousy must be getting the better of him.

"Assuming she's still in Scotland." Jeff's tone was dry. Kingsley was upset and trying to bait him with this sudden reference to his past love. They had not spoken of Amy for years. He was completely blind to Kingsley's desire for him. But he saw suddenly that his friend might not wish his position usurped. Ronald de Souza, another of their boyhood friends, had emigrated to Melbourne nearly a decade earlier. He was offering Jeff an easy transition; a place in his legal firm.

Kingsley sighed. It seemed that half their social circle had, or were about to, emigrate to Melbourne. He could not plumb the depths of such an enigma. Of course, Jeff and Greta with their Dutch Burgher heritage would have no difficulty being accepted as suitable immigrants by the Australians. His own mother was a Portuguese Burgher, his skin was perhaps a shade too tanned; even so, he might still pass the Australians' curious race test and be allowed in. Yet, many of his closest friends and relatives would not be, no matter their degree of education or sophistication, merely because of the colour of their skin. He could not understand or abide anyone wanting to go to such a place. There were so many other options. "So, the "White Australia Policy" is no deterrent? Had your genealogy done at the DBU as yet?" There was uncharacteristic bitterness in his voice.

"Kingsley, this has to happen. I'd stay if I could, but there's no future here." Jeff looked at his friend. "You know I can't go back to Britain, or the States for that matter." He smiled a play-ful smile. "I won't survive the cold."

"What can I say to such a compelling argument?" Kings-ley lifted the letter and folded his slender body into the chair on the opposite side of Jeff's desk. He sat slightly forward, on alert. He held the sheets of paper with their elegant script in his hand, and struggled to bring the message on them into focus.

Ronald had always been persuasive, adept at life in a way he felt he never could be. He knew that Jeff considered them both his closest friends, and would have liked nothing better than that they feel the same way about each other. But it was not to be, his own jealousy was too strong to allow it. Ronald was nonplussed by his reserve, had always tolerated him for the sake of Jeff's company. He listened to the slow rhythmic creaking of the overhead fan as it circled slowly, and felt it gently shift the air around him to bring some coolness as it wafted across the wet patch on his back where his shirt clung to his skin. He was tempted to take the letter and retreat into his own office. To study at leisure the missive that might end life as he knew it.

He and Jeff had been side by side for so many years, in so many ways. They had studied law together in Colombo, then gone to Britain to gain further postgraduate qualifications at the same time; he in London and Jeff in Edinburgh. He had been Jeff's main support at the time of his parents' death and in his decision to leave his Scottish lover and return to Ceylon. He had been best man at his wedding and a constant visitor in his home, befriended by his wife. They played tennis every Saturday. He joined the family on holiday at times. He was godfather to Jeff's daughter. It was all about to end. "Have you spoken to Greta about this?"

"Not a word. I didn't want to open the conversation until I had a chance of convincing her." Jeff's face clouded as he stared past his friend. "I've been procrastinating terribly, Kingsley. You know there is nothing I want more than to stay. But not with what's coming. There's no place for us here. Condemn the Australians if you will, but the Sinhalese want us gone. Our religion is not their religion. Our skin is too light for their taste. A few hundred years here is nothing in their eyes, gives us no right to call Ceylon our home. I pity the Tamils with Mrs Bandaranaike in power. There'll be more race riots, more marginalisation, it's going to happen. I should have left after the coup failed two years ago. I just haven't been able to bear the thought of going. Leila starts school next year. Maybe if they hadn't changed the national language from English to Sinhalese it would be different. I don't want her to do all her schooling in Sinhalese. It will come to that, even at religious private schools. Mark my words! We have to go."

Kingsley stared at him doggedly. "Many of our friends are Sinhalese or Tamil."

Jeff eyed him, wondering if he was feigning naivety or struggling to face the inevitable, as he himself had been for so long. "And Christian, and Westernised! I can imagine them leaving too, if they could. As we lose our standing here, as more of us go, things will get worse for those who stay. I'm sure of it. The hatred will escalate. Have you read Sirisena? Do you think I want my daughter seen as the personification of evil when she grows up—the loose Burgher siren that every good Sinhala man must denounce to prove his virtue? Do I want to live in a Ceylon where she is vilified by those who agree with him?"

"Of course not! But he's retaliating. We're just as prejudiced. Are you a Dutch or Portuguese Burgher? When did your last relative come here from Europe or England? Did your cousin marry someone Sinhalese or Tamil? Are we as good as the British? Need I go on? We've had it our way, it was never going to last with independence. We're such a tiny proportion of the population and we've held so many of the choice positions. Your father was a judge, mine the deputy commissioner of police. Of course, the Sinhalese want us gone! The British used us, our desire to be them. We were their greatest allies here.

We didn't have to find a new place when the Dutch left, just lapped up the privilege, took it all for granted. Our time has passed and we don't like it, that's all!"

Kingsley's long intelligent face was flushed with emotion; he was sitting forward in his seat emphasising his words with each fluent movement of his hands. The time had come to be honest, there was no point in anything less. Jeff was leaving. He may never get this chance again. He felt a familiar surge of self-hatred, for he knew that this was all he would dare; a dispute about politics that carried some of his anger and disappointment, never a mention of what lay in his heart.

"I didn't know you were so aligned with the Sinhala nationalists." Jeff's tone was dry.

Kingsley straightened in his seat. "Perhaps I have some sympathy for people who've gone unheeded, had so little agency in their own country for so long."

"For heaven's sake, Kingsley! When did you become so saintly?" Jeff's anger kindled. He knew that racial tensions were increasing in unpredictable ways and violence could break out at any moment, even in Colombo. The militancy of the Sinhala left led by radicalised Buddhist priests meant that no one was safe. His tone was suddenly searing. "Solomon Bandaranaike was assassinated when he was prime minister by a Buddhist priest! Despite his conversion from Christianity to Buddhism, and his espousal of Sinhala socialism, at the expense of everyone of other ethnic origins, including many of his friends, who all think Ceylon is their home!" He rarely expressed hatred for what he saw as the wilful destruction of his homeland. It was close to being turned upon his friend. He looked away. He was surprised by the intensity of his own reaction and struggled to understand Kingsley's position instead.

Kingsley looked up, his face solemn; a mask that hid the depth of his grief and despair at what was unfolding. "I'm not aligned with them. I like to think I'm a realist."

Jeff considered his friend. There was truth in everything he said. Yet he was dismissing their world, their right to a sense of national identity, as though it had no depth, no meaning. Jeff knew that having a child had made his decision to leave much harder, more complex. None of this current reality was what he wanted for Leila. What he did want was the Ceylon of his own childhood. He had tarried to show her, to let her taste its richness and beauty. Yet living through his identification with her, he had found it all the harder to contemplate leaving. He knew he could adapt and may even thrive elsewhere. Yet this island was in every way his home, and so he had lingered. He softened. "Are you going to leave, Kingsley?"

Strange, so strange they had never had this conversation, though it had been brewing, inevitable, for years. They had spent their days together, each knowing somewhere this day would come; now it had. "Why don't you come to Australia too?"

Kingsley laughed. "No, no not for me. You can give Ronald my best. I think, in time, I'll head to Britain. Still a few sad souls who might welcome me back, I hope."

London, such a different world for him; the place where he had relished his anonymity, finally felt some freedom to be himself, to explore his sexuality. He had undoubtedly risked jail there too for his sexual preference, but in England at this very moment there were people working to decriminalise homosexuality, friends and lovers who wrote him of a brewing change, a time of greater freedom that hovered on the brink of realisation. It was so different from the constant prying eyes and gossiping circles of Burgher society that confronted him daily in Colombo, a circle in which he was always known and so dared nothing. He had never contemplated taking the risk to explore any other island communities where the fairness of his skin would immediately marginalise and define him.

He had abandoned London only after encouraging Jeff to leave Scotland and return to Ceylon at the time of his parents' death. He had felt compelled to go with him, spend whatever time he could with him, knowing always he would lose him one day. But by now Burghers had been leaving Ceylon in legions for more than a decade, and both of them would suffer dearly for their tardiness in going. The restrictions on taking money out of the island were extreme, while only a few years ago each might have taken his wealth with him. Jeff appeared to know nothing of his homosexuality, the secret reality that defined his life. Yet, might he at some subliminal level suspect? This suggestion that he come to Australia was late in coming and weak at best, if not an empty gesture. Kingsley felt his body sink deeper into the chair. He still clung to the letter, his face morose.

"Come on, cheer up! It's not the Cuban Missile Crisis! It's just our world that's ending. How about lunch at the Pagoda, my shout?" Jeff rose from his chair and walked around his desk, a sudden energy in his step. He stood directly in front of his friend.

Kingsley looked up at him, as always taken by his vitality and physical presence. Still he felt despondent. "It will be full of the same crowd that will be at the party tonight. I don't think I'm up for it twice in one day." He sparked up. "Though I could come now, and forget about the Leembruggens' do?"

"Not on your life! Greta will be impossible if you're not there to dance the night away with her!" The amusement in Jeff's voice vied with something else; subtle, barely perceptible, but undeniably present.

Kingsley sighed inwardly. Had his ruse worked too well? Did Jeff fear that he was secretly in love with his wife? He knew that Greta believed this to be true and liked the idea. She was emotionally strangely astute at times. She would have picked up his intensity and passion for a certainty, in a way Jeff never could. It was far safer that she believed it directed at her; a flattering crush or some vaguely tragic unrequited love, never to be expressed because of his loyalty to his best friend. It would satisfy her vanity and sense of romance, while his true feelings would repulse her, of that he was sure. Would they repulse Jeff too? It was a risk he would never take. He knew he could not survive the pain of such a rejection.

* * *

They entered the room together, moving with a natural affinity; a symmetry born of years of close relating, that neither was aware of. They were the same height. Both tall and lean, though Jeff was the more muscular and masculine of the two by far.

"Ah, the beautiful men have arrived." Edna Misso had somehow insinuated herself between them and taken each by the arm as she greeted them near the entrance, then guided them into the large, noisy restaurant. She had seen them deep in conversation as they entered the restaurant, had left her seat to come at them from the side, as if by chance. It was all so seamless, yet observed by many. "You know you were the two most eligible bachelors in Colombo for many a year."

"Many a year ago, Edna!" Jeff was irritated by her. He had dated her briefly in his early twenties. He could not remember if Kingsley had ever done so. Anyone Kingsley dated, he dated briefly. True, both of them had a reputation for dating many different women in their youth, but he had been married for seven years now, while Kingsley had never found the right woman, never settled down. He suspected some deep affair of the heart in London, that Kingsley had not deigned to share with him. Perhaps that was unfair. Kingsley always had a far deeper nature. Things got to him in some different way. He had appreciated Kingsley's support immensely through his own emotional trials in the UK. He should ask no more. Strange how this woman always managed to insert herself between them, emotionally as well as physically. He realised that he had found himself questioning Kingsley's friendship in odd ways before in her presence, although he was never sure how or why this happened.

Jeff took Edna's hand and removed it from his arm, disconnecting himself from her physically as he attempted to follow a waiter to the table he had booked. But she stubbornly clung to Kingsley's arm and came with them. Jeff stopped before reaching the table. "I'm sorry, Edna. This is a business lunch. What say we catch up this evening?" He had no idea if she was invited to the Leembruggens' party, but he knew she would never admit it if she was not.

"Alright, I'll leave you to your business, as long as you each promise me a dance tonight?" Her voice was high pitched and coquettish. Kingsley inclined his head ever so slightly, while Jeff began circling around tables to reach the table where their waiter stood. Edna made do and hurried back to her sister and aunt seated at the front of the restaurant.

"What is wrong with that woman?" Jeff sat down abruptly and pulled his serviette on to his lap in exasperation before the waiter could place it there. He took the offered menu and began to study it, but closed it rapidly and handed it back to the waiter. "Just the usual. Rice and curry and whisky for two."

Kingsley looked at his friend with feigned amusement. "Guess she just never got over you, like so many of the rest! You can hardly criticise her for wishing she were in Greta's place."

Jeff blanched momentarily. "Never, Kingsley, never! Not even in jest!" He laughed suddenly, an unexpected laugh, that carried in it a note of sadness. "We came here to celebrate after all, didn't we? There are some people I won't miss, and others … ." The waiter had already placed the whisky before them. Jeff raised his glass. "To the next phase."

* * *

Kingsley sat at his desk staring at the brief in front of him. Try as he might he could not take it in. A simple land dispute,

61

his bread and butter. He watched a gecko as it neared a crack in the wall just below the point where the wall and ceiling met. It stopped, frozen in time, like some grey-brown stain or patch of mildew on the plaster, then jerked forward suddenly and disappeared into the crack. The creaking hum of the fan as it rocked and circled above was now strangely soothing. Just two shots of whisky, why did his head ache so? But no more than his chest. This was not indigestion. The first time he had felt this deep ache behind his breastbone he had feared for his life, thought he must be having a heart attack at a premature age, as his mother's brother had done. That was the night Jeff had rung him from Edinburgh, so eager to tell him he had fallen in love with Amy, might consider a life in Scotland after all, for her sake.

At Jeff's urging he had caught the train to Edinburgh to meet her, only a few weekends later, in early springtime. The three of them had made the climb to Arthur's Seat; with parklands giving way to craggy rising hills as they climbed further, then to cliffsides covered in lush sage and green, and gorse bushes afire with yellow flowers among the remnants of the morning's snowfall. The view had changed with each turning of the path, enlarging, diminishing until there before them lay the Firth of Forth, the distant snow-capped mountains and the marvellous glistening old stone city. Amazing Amy, laughing with the pleasure of introducing these men of the tropics to the beauty of the world she inhabited, eager to meet Jeff's best friend, to share their joy with him.

He had sensed at once what Jeff loved: her infectious play-fulness, her keen and determined mind, her natural kindness. She far outstripped him in every way. There was no way for him to compete. Even more, he had seen that she was fast becoming Jeff's best friend and confidante, that he would soon be redundant. But there had been limitations, drawbacks that could be leveraged. She, like Jeff, was an only child and her parents did not favour the prospect of her moving thousands of miles away to the tropics. She seemed in any case ill-suited for such a life with her auburn hair and pale, freckled complexion. He knew this was nonsense; his cousin was a redhead who used a parasol at midday and managed perfectly in Colombo. He had needed to believe he was somehow considering Amy's best interests as well, in order to prise Jeff away, for she was a rare and lovely person, one he could not help but admire.

He had not thought of Amy at any length for years. She would occasionally pop into his mind when Greta did something particularly gauche or thoughtless, as a tiny prick of guilty conscience. Jeff's sudden, unexpected choice of such a limited young woman for his wife had suited him very well. It had bought him a few years. He breathed slowly, his breath did not catch, but the ache persisted. He would need to find a way to see this through, to appear normal, disappointed perhaps, but not unduly so.

He had a sudden longing to hurt Jeff, show him what jealousy might feel like. Should he see how far he could take things with Greta? He knew nothing of her reputation prior to her marriage to Jeff. He had given Jeff his word not to enquire into her past at the time of their meeting. He had honoured that promise and extended it. He never countenanced any hint of rumour or gossip about Greta. To those around the three of them it made him appear both her champion and Jeff's most loyal friend.

She clearly enjoyed flirting with him, but never more than that, and had been entirely loyal to Jeff as far as he knew. Perhaps he could make some show of his sadness at losing her. Was it worth the effort? Would having Jeff dislike or hate him make the coming parting any less difficult? No, he realised he did not have it in him, and it would probably only make things worse. What hurt him most was the fact that Jeff had not asked his advice in this life changing, country changing decision. He had played his hand with Ronald too close to give him the slightest in.

He gazed once more at the brief on the table before him. The words blurred into each other. He could not focus. He stopped trying and sat back, let the air from the fan waft over his upturned face. The truth dawned on him slowly as he sat there: Jeff did not trust him now, while once he had trusted him most of all. It might have something to do with his advice about Amy and something to do with how he related to Greta. But he would assuredly lose Jeff to Ronald, who would take the one true place he had occupied, that of best friend and work partner. There was nothing he could do to stop it. He had destroyed his relationship with the man he loved more than anyone else in the world. The ache in his chest felt unbearable. It was time for him to let go.

* * *

"I just don't understand it!" George Wambeek's round, good-natured face was morose. "What do these chaps want?" His collar was too tight and the folds of his neck were trapped by it. Beads of perspiration coalesced and began to create a rim of dampness there.

Jeff wanted to ask him to loosen his tie and undo his top button but resisted the urge. George was struggling enough already, no need to draw attention to his physical discomfort as well. Jeff kept his voice measured. There was nothing for it but plain speech. "They're after your best plantation, the real question is what do you want to do about it?"

George was in his late forties. His hair was greying at the temples. Their parents had been friends. Jeff remembered being a boy and visiting Matara to stay on the very plantation they were discussing. George had been a young man, in his late teens or early twenties, slim and energetic. He had given Jeff his first tennis lesson on the tennis courts there. The house and the gardens were so lovely, with a view that fell away to the river.

"You know my mother loved that place, more than anywhere else we owned. It came from her side of the family. Her grandfather left it to her, made my uncle Gerard furious." He laughed. "But she'd loved it as a girl, I guess her grandfather knew." His voice grew sadder. "They're trying to force me out you know. Suddenly no one wants to work my land. If I don't agree to their terms, all of my plantations may be under threat."

"Have you thought of approaching the authorities?" Jeff knew he had to ask; George was here as his client, but he recognised how disingenuous he sounded. Nothing but further intimidation would come of such an enquiry. He sighed deeply, and opted for directness. His time here was limited. He could not bear the thought that his last advice to George could be construed as some self-serving platitude. Their relationship demanded more. "Forget that I asked, George, we both know where that might lead."

George looked at him with relief and then sadness. "Just don't know who to trust anymore. They're going to rip the whole place out, planning to build a hotel complex. Fred Peiris told me. Went to school with the fellow and he stands there and tells me as though we're chatting about some bridge game." His face was flushed. He looked past Jeff at a painting of palm trees lining a sunlit beach that hung on the wall behind him. "Should have left you know. Should have left years ago. I couldn't bear to go. I've never been away from here." His voice was plaintive. "Could you imagine it; living somewhere away from the sea and the jungle? Somewhere with no elephants?" His eyes widened. "No monkeys?"

Jeff remembered then just how enthusiastic George had always been about wildlife. How much he had hated the hunting parties his father had led to bag duck and snipe, and how he had railed at so-called bird-watchers who participated in the sport. It was the only time he had seen him upset, until now.

65

George steadied himself and looked at Jeff. "But you have been overseas, haven't you? Studied in England?"

"Scotland … a very different place." Jeff's eyes held a far-away look for a moment. "Certainly, no elephants or monkeys, no jungles, no sunbirds either, but some wonderful seabirds and wild empty places … that certainly had their allure."

George laughed gently. "First love?"

Jeff looked at him in surprise. He had never thought George perceptive. But then who ever talked about what was really going on? All conversation was a variation on the theme of endless superficiality. He had kept things light ever since his parents died, since he had abandoned Scotland and Amy. He realised that life's reality had been missing since he came back home, missing most of the time, but not today. He felt annoyed with Kingsley. He was the one who had brought Amy into their conversation and into his mind again. He had hidden her away in a sealed place, or so he thought. Yet, here she was again, springing to mind, visible to someone who had never known her, but someone who had known him as a boy, known his parents. He looked at George; they were both hurting. His voice was soft. "Yes, she was quite lovely."

"Not a wild beauty like Greta then?"

Jeff recoiled silently. It was inconceivable that George was attacking Greta's reputation. He must think this some form of compliment. He responded in kind. "No one is quite like Greta!"

"You're not thinking of going, are you, Jeff?"

He was perceptive, certainly. "You're something of a mind reader, George. I've underestimated you!" Jeff leant forward. "I am leaving. I just have to convince my wife. I heard from Ronald de Souza today, it's pretty much settled."

"So? … Melbourne? Kingsley going with you?"

Jeff looked surprised. "What? No, I asked him but he has other plans."

"Well, I hope they include staying for some time at least. I'll need his help. I'm going to have to see if there's a way to safeguard anything I own." He sighed. "We won't be leaving. I know how to run my estates and that's about it. Not much of a transferable occupation, as far as I can make out. The fact that we have no children clinches it." He laughed but there was no humour in it. "I was going to leave it all to Louisa's nephew, but he's heading for Canada next month." He looked up and met Jeff's eyes. "It's a hell of a thing, isn't it? I'm glad my mother didn't live to see it; the end of the world she knew and loved."

The thought had never entered Jeff's mind, but it did now, with a strange solemnity and force. "Yes, I'm very glad that neither of my parents lived to see it." They sat together in silence, both transported to a moment from many years ago when the parents they loved were alive and playful and life seemed to offer the unending promise that it would continue just as it was.

* * *

Jeff checked his watch. He had promised Greta to be home early, and he wanted to see Leila before they left for the Leembruggens' party, which he had been warned was being held earlier than was usual. He opened his diary. Half an hour's break and then two more clients for the afternoon. No one he could cancel. A will to be signed and the finalising of documents for a property transfer. Both matters better completed. He struggled with the thought of seeing anyone else. Even stranger, he did not want to leave his office and risk running into Kingsley. They would see each other at the party tonight and somehow that seemed enough.

Kingsley was upset with him, for his decision to leave, for not being informed of it. Odd, how he just hadn't thought about

Kingsley while exploring a possible new life in Melbourne and a partnership with Ronald. It was only now that it dawned on him how strange this was. It was as if he had somehow felt that Kingsley was in on it, part of the plan, though not included. He had been deeply surprised at the intensity of Kingsley's reaction to his news. Had he been afraid that Kingsley would hint at it with Greta before he was ready to tell her?

He would sort things out with him. There had never been any problem between them before and he saw no reason why this should be different. He and Kingsley wished the best for each other. It was a given in their relationship. The course each of their lives was taking might diverge from this point, but their friendship would stand the test of time and distance, of that he was sure. His friendship with Ronald certainly had.

His mind moved away from his friend. What he really needed to do was focus on Greta, and how best to tell her. The thing was out. He had spoken of it explicitly with two others in Colombo today. He must let her know the same day or risk not being forgiven. He knew how her mind worked. For others to know before her would be seen as a betrayal. If she found out the same day, the exact timeline of events would blur and become irrelevant. Any further delay would remain a source of irritation and resentment to rile and tug at her in the future. He knew also that he must find a way to include her in the decision, make it as much hers as his own.

How was that possible? The truth was that neither of them wanted to leave. He had simply been the first to realise that they had no future here and no other choice. He began to replay his conversation with Kingsley but stopped himself. No point getting caught in his rage at the madness of what was going on, at the destruction of the country he loved. Greta did not want to hear the detail. He must find another way to convince her that it was not wise to stay, and that Ceylon was no longer the place to raise their daughter.

He checked his watch and pulled a file towards him. He opened it. This was going to be difficult. Rohan van Cuylenberg was a successful businessman, a contemporary of his father's. He must be in his early seventies. His father and Rohan had never been friends, although they moved in the same circles. There had always been a tension between them. Jeff had sensed it as a child at social gatherings. The two men had pointedly avoided each other at close quarters, in the same drawing room. He had never seen his father behave this way with anyone else, had never thought to ask him why. By the time such a thing might have occurred to him he no longer accompanied his parents on social outings. He suddenly remembered his father in a way he had not done for years; he recalled his face vividly, almost felt his presence. A wave of immense sadness buffeted him. He had been completely preoccupied with his own life and then suddenly there had been no time for questions, even the mundane. His parents had died instantly, in a car crash, while he was in Scotland.

He caught himself and tried to focus on the file. He longed that something today could be easy. This would not be. It had been his choice to accept. He had somehow felt compelled to take up the task, as much by curiosity as to why he had been chosen, as anything else. What he had found unsettled him. The instructions had been mailed to him and were precise, but the content was complex; with assets here and abroad, and beneficiaries that included a wife and two mistresses and both legitimate and illegitimate children.

He heard the door open and close in the anteroom and his secretary laugh as she welcomed someone. There was a knock on the door, a short rap, his secretary's signal that she was about to usher in a client. The door opened and Gimhani smiled as she held the door open. Jeff smiled back at her and was annoyed at how the elderly man who entered his office brushed past her as he did so. He was immaculately dressed and walked with a cane that was clearly there to complete the outfit. An anglophile! Jeff had never consciously given anyone that title. He noted his annoyance and decided to temper it.

"Ah, Thomas van Buuren's boy! Last saw you when you were in nappies!"

"A tad later I think, unless my memory is remarkable!"

"Remember me, do you?" Rohan van Cuylenberg's face wore a wry smile.

"Yes, you're the only person I ever saw my father treat with obvious dislike."

"Touché!" The older man mimed a lob at the net, then reached forward and extended his hand to Jeff who stood behind his desk. Jeff hesitated, just for a moment, then took the offered hand and shook it briefly, surprised that the handshake too was not turned into some test of dominance as he half anticipated.

Rohan laughed. "So, he taught you a thing or two after all. Good, good. I want that will to be airtight. No room for anyone to contest it!" He looked at Jeff. "You're no doubt wondering why I asked you to prepare it? Truth is, I disliked your father far more than he disliked me, and with greater cause. But the man knew his stuff when it came to the law. No doubt about that."

"Regrettably, my father had no chance to teach me anything about the law Mr van Cuylenberg. He died before I was able to return here and practise it."

"Nonsense! I'm talking about the stuff in your bones, you know, his immense nobility and doing the right thing, and all that!" He stared at Jeff strangely. "He didn't have anyone contesting his will for example, did he?"

"No, I'm an only child."

"My point exactly. And you can be sure of that, can't you? Unlike my unfortunate children who are in for a big shock once I'm gone!" He laughed with deep pleasure.

Jeff sat down and examined the papers in front of him, then handed them to Rohan who was still standing, appraising him intensely. Rohan took them and lowered himself into the leather chair on the other side of the desk and began to read. The same chair in which Kingsley had sat that morning arguing with him as never before. Jeff was surprised by the thought. He needed to focus. This man was up to something. But he had no inkling what it was.

"Yes, it's all exactly as I wanted it. Excellent. You know they're a mangy lot. Likely to cause trouble." He read on.

Jeff looked at him. He seemed both content and excited, if the two were possible simultaneously. "It might help if you make your reasoning more explicit. A clause or two about why you are leaving something to a particular person goes a long way, if you're anticipating a challenge."

Rohan laughed deeply. "Oh, it will be challenged alright! Do I want to make it hard for them? Yes, maybe. But who do I want to make it hardest for? Those who are in for a shock and think it's all theirs? Or those who I've told some element of the truth and expect to be included? One thing's for sure, I won't be here to see it." He smiled broadly. "They might all just come knocking at your door!"

"Sadly no, not unless they plan a sea voyage. I'm leaving for Australia in the not too distant future." Number three! At least no chance of Greta ever speaking to this obnoxious man!

"I see, not all my plans will play out then."

"You can't be serious? You want to embroil me in some dispute between your wife, your mistresses and your children because you disliked my father, who died years ago?"

"Why not? He stole my fiancée, the woman I truly loved and with whom I'm sure I would have led a very different life." The older man's face wore a look of absolute certainty.

Jeff shuddered inwardly. "My mother was engaged to you?"

"Just like him, sanctimonious, exuding distaste! The image of the man!" He stared at Jeff but could not hold his gaze. He was sitting forward, his chest puffed out. He sat back in the chair and seemed to deflate suddenly. He looked away.

71

His face was drawn. When he spoke again, his previous bluster was absent, his voice strangely subdued. "You look like her. Seen you about. It's the only reason I came. Here let me sign it. You witness it." They signed the documents in silence. Rohan van Cuylenberg stood to go. "You might have been my son you know, had things been different."

Jeff watched him leave, trying to fathom such a bizarre comment, on this most strange and unnerving of days.

* * *

Kingsley was getting nowhere. He shut the brief in front of him and decided to head home. He stood and lifted his suit jacket off the back of his chair, slung it over his arm and walked out of his office closing the door behind him. Ghimani looked up from behind her desk and smiled at him. "Mister Jeff just finished with his client if you want speak to him. Next one won't be here for fifteen minutes I think."

"Thanks, Ghimani." He had hoped Jeff would be busy with someone and he could simply leave. But he always said good-bye, if it were possible; she would think it strange if he did not. Then he remembered that he had driven Jeff in that morning and would ordinarily drive him home. He knocked on Jeff's door and poked his head in. "I'm calling it a day."

Jeff looked up. "Love to come with you, but I've got one more. Don't wait about, I'll get a cab." He seemed distracted. "It's been the oddest day." He suddenly became animated. "Just get there on time tonight, won't you Kingsley? It's starting early. I'll have to talk to Greta about my plans this evening, before or after the party. In either case I'll need your help. Dancing always puts her in a good mood!"

"Of course! Ever happy to oblige! See you this evening." Kingsley's voice was strained.

"Great, see you at the Leembruggens." Jeff smiled vaguely in his friend's direction and pulled his last brief towards him.

Kingsley banged the door shut as he headed out of their office building.

He needed to get home. He'd had enough of everyone. He ached for a long bath. He drove through the bustling traffic of the Pettah on automatic as he made his way to Wellewatta and the sanctuary of his home. He lived in the annex of his aunt and uncle's house; it was a self-contained flat really with its own driveway. He was fortunate in that their house servants took care of it as well as the main house, and their cook made him meals whenever he wanted them. He paid a nominal rent and was a great favourite of theirs. At times, they tried to matchmake for him, but in truth enjoyed the fact that he was still single, adept at cards and fond of their company. Both of their children had died in early childhood; one of typhoid and the other after an epileptic fit that came on with a high temperature. They were overjoyed when Kingsley decided to take their offer and move in with them on his return from England.

Kingsley lay in his bath and pondered his life in Colombo. His father had died in his teens and his mother had remarried not long after. He'd never got on with his stepfather, although both his younger siblings did. He had found himself estranged from his mother, brother and sister as a result and seldom visited any of them. His family had tolerated his behaviour until the birth of a niece and a nephew in recent years. When he showed no interest in meeting or getting to know this youngest generation, he had been met with marked anger and resentment at any family gathering he managed to make himself attend.

There was nothing for him in Colombo, except for his aunt and uncle's affection for him and his relationship with Jeff, and he was leaving. Jeff was leaving. He began to cry; deep racking sobs. It stunned him. He never cried. He slid down slowly in the bath; the water encircled his face, he closed his eyes and let the momentum continue until his head was completely under water. He slid further still and lay on the bottom of the tub. He opened his eyes and looked up at the light shifting as the water lapped gently above him, displaced by the motion of his body as he'd submerged. The light and the water seemed alive and strangely soothing. He could not cry down here. He no longer wanted to.

He sat up abruptly and shook his head, shaking the water out of his ears. He could give the party a miss, stay home this evening. He did not have to inflict any more pain on himself. He had coped with grief and loss before. He had lost his whole family after his father died. Jeff had made his plans and it was likely that he and Greta would be gone in six months tops. He must decide whether he stayed to watch this departure or left first himself. It was an empowering thought. He climbed out of the bath and towelled his body dry vigorously. He'd play his role tonight, then plan his own departure.

CHAPTER FOUR

Colombo 1954

Greta hurried through the school gates and began the walk home. She worked hard to stay in the shade as much as she could, to the point of crossing and recrossing the street, dodging the traffic and ignoring the honking horns of irritated drivers. With her hair in braids she was unremarkable among the throng of girls pouring out of the school in their crisp white uniforms and green ties. Some were being picked up by parents or drivers but many were on foot as she was, mostly walking in small groups, their numbers decreasing the further away she got from her school.

Albert loved her fair complexion, called her his golden girl. She got excited at the thought of him, of just talking to him. It was all that was possible since he had gone away. What would it actually be like to see him again? He was coming back to Colombo in another week. She had only dared call him once at his plantation in all the time he had been away. He had asked her to come to his office in Colombo next Tuesday. She trembled at the thought. She feared her mother suspected something, but it was not likely: her mother was always too busy to notice anything real about her. Cynthia was the true cause for concern. But luckily, she was absorbed with her teaching degree and her relationship with Ernest. She had far less time for the constant scrutiny, negative observations and complaints that had plagued the years they had spent together at the same school. Greta was nothing but a source of disappointment to her sister, that much was clear.

She was nearly home. Why was she thinking about Cynthia at all? With any luck, Cynthia would marry the very earnest and boring Ernest Jansz. She smiled at her own wit. The sooner the better. But that would only be a good thing if those two went and lived with his relatives. Heaven forbid they should want to move into the tiny house that she shared with her mother and Cynthia and their servant girl Elly.

She shuddered involuntarily at the thought of anyone else living there, let alone the well-meaning Ernest. He always tried his best to be friendly but she found his attempts to involve her in conversation achingly dull. Were books or politics really all that he and Cynthia ever discussed, or just the only conversation he foisted on her? He was four years older than Cynthia, who was three years older than her. Was this all a man of twenty-three really had to discuss? He was gauche and clumsy with her. She would turn and find him staring at her. She hated it. It made Cynthia somehow dislike her more, which was most unfair, as it had nothing to do with how she related to him.

She had decided from the first time Cynthia brought him home to be on her very best behaviour. She didn't flirt and she didn't start any topic of conversation that she knew would bring disapproval from Cynthia or her mother. When neither of these things seemed to make any difference, she stayed in her room as much as possible whenever Ernest came to visit.

It was decided. It would be a fine thing for Cynthia to marry Ernest and leave their home, but they simply could not move in. In any case there was nowhere to put them. They could hardly spend all their time huddled together in Cynthia's room, keeping quiet and keeping away from the drawing room, the way she and Cynthia had to live. The drawing room was converted into her mother's showroom and workspace. Her mother's customers were always visiting, to decide on dress designs and choose fabrics, or have fittings behind the beautifully carved wooden screen that her mother had somehow salvaged and retained from her own family home and far more affluent childhood. Greta sighed. Such a shame they'd lost their wealth. She'd have much more chance of luring Albert away from his ugly old wife if she was wealthy. She was sure of it.

She rounded the corner and headed down her street, stopping suddenly beneath a large flamboyant tree in bloom. She looked at the beautiful red flowers above her and at those lying withered, scattered on the ground. She tried her hardest to stop the rage that was brewing in her. It would do her no good to go home to her mother this way. But it always happened. As soon as she thought about better luck, or better times, this always followed; her desperate anger at the loss of her father. Up would surge the voice that tormented her, that said her father had died because her mother stole her away from him, died before she could ever see him again.

She saw a car pull up outside her home and a woman get out of the passenger's door and walk inside. Good. One of her mother's customers almost certainly. She could make her way to her room without any scrutiny or any useless questions about how her day at school had been, without risking yet another fight with her mother. These would erupt out of nowhere. It was hard to work out what they were about. But she knew that when they happened she hated her mother and wished more than anything that she could move out, that Albert would ask her to marry him, that she could live in his big house or go away for the weekend with him to one of his rubber and coconut estates near Kandy.

The fact that she was sixteen and still at school, and he forty-two and married, made no difference at such times of desperation. She longed to escape. Longed to leave the confines of a life that trapped her in a house with her mother and sister, who she was sure had never begun to like her, leave aside any question of love. But Alfred loved her. She knew he simply must.

77

He had never come right out and said it. But why else had he made such an effort to see her, risked his wife finding out, maybe even the end of his marriage? Now, that would be a wonderful thing indeed!

They had met two months ago at her Aunt Inez's house. It was not a place that she enjoyed visiting ordinarily. Yet, she knew she had to go. The whole family, and she in particular, were under obligation to Aunt Inez and Uncle Edward, who had taken them in at a time of dire need. She had stayed on with them while her mother and Cynthia went ahead to make a home for them all. That was the story. She was supposed to feel grateful to them. But she had worked out that this must have been at the time when her mother left her father in the hill country and moved them all down to Colombo. Maybe if Inez and Edward hadn't put them up her mother might have thought differently about leaving, might have tried to sort things out with her father instead. She imagined countless other ways in which her life could have worked out so much better, if only her father had been with her.

She had no memory at all of the time she had spent with Inez and Edward as a young child, though she had been told that she lived with them for over a year until she started school. All she knew was that she had a sense of dread whenever she came near their house and often felt sick and found it difficult to eat the food they offered her. Yet, she forced it down, so as not to seem rude or bad natured. She was sure that this made no difference, to her mother at least, that no matter how hard she tried nothing she did would ever convince her mother that she was anything other than bad. What Aunt Inez or Uncle Edward thought of her was of no real importance at all. She was just playing the civility game, doing what her mother deemed the correct thing to do in the circumstances.

Albert and his wife had been visiting too that day. His wife was so pleased to meet her mother, had been meaning to come and see her about making a special gown. Albert had asked her to show him the garden. Aunty Inez had encouraged her to do it, and she had of course felt obliged to do so. How strange that she had been annoyed at the thought. But he had seemed so old to her at that first meeting. Until of course they were in the garden together and he had begun to talk of magical things; of his plantations and their beauty, of distant countries he had visited. He talked to her as if she were a woman, an equal. It made her feel like she was someone who mattered, not the one who was always a nuisance or causing trouble simply by existing.

Two months ago, and so much excitement and longing between then and now. Her life had changed. He had picked her up in his car after school a week after that first meeting, must have followed her some distance before doing so, to wisely get away from any prying eyes. He had told her how beautiful she was, how sad and unhappy he was in his marriage, how she made him remember all the things he loved in life, brought new meaning to his otherwise dreary existence. He had held her hand. He had stroked her cheek. He had given her the most beautiful little emerald pendant. She had hidden it away.

He had preoccupied her waking thoughts and most of her dreams ever since, though he had to go away to somewhere near Kandy to supervise some major work going on at one of his plantations there. He had given her his phone number up there as well as the number for his office in Colombo. They had met once more, briefly, before he left, in a tea house not far from her home. It had felt so forbidden, so exciting. They had sat together and had tea and cakes, he acting as though he was some relative of hers until they walked outside, then pulling her beneath an overhanging tree. He had felt her breasts and touched her bottom and kissed her hard on the mouth, then laughed and pushed her away. "You'll have to wait till I get back!"

What exactly had he meant by that? She felt a deep plea-surable sensation between her legs and got quite hot at the

79

thought. She had to find a way to go and see him next Tuesday if she could. But they would need to be careful. She'd have to wear something other than her school uniform, then they wouldn't be so conspicuous together. That meant she'd have to take an outfit with her to school. Where could she change? Where could she leave her school bag? She dared not tell any of her friends or involve them by going to one of their houses. No one was able to keep such a thing secret. It was simply too exciting.

She entered the house quietly by the side door, hoping her mother would not hear her, that she could get to her room in time to change and go out once more. Maybe she could try to call him at his plantation again. She longed to hear his voice. But would he get angry if she called before next Tuesday, the time he had asked her to call? He had never been angry with her so far. But people always got angry with her in the end. She did not want to risk it.

"Greta, is that you?" Her mother's voice was eager, as always in the company of strangers.

"Yes, Mum." Her tone was flat. The show, the pretence of affection, how she hated it. Yet, she complied, did not dare use the abrasive tone she often used to discourage her mother from asking more, not with a customer in the house.

"Can you come in here for a moment please? I need a hand."

Greta dropped her school bag on the floor in the kitchen. She felt a new steely determination. She would not fight with her mother or Cynthia anymore. There was no need to. She was no longer trapped in their meagre world. Albert loved her and this made anything possible. Her life might turn out wonderfully after all.

She walked slowly into the front room. Her mother was pinning a jet-black gown trimmed with silver on a large, shapely woman who had her back turned to them. It would be stunning, Greta was sure of it. Her mother had a flare for this. Such a shame it meant behaving like a servant to these people, being obsequious, pandering to their whims and expectations. The woman turned. It was his wife. Greta blanched and stood still.

"Rosemary, this is my younger girl Greta. I think you met her at Inez and Edward's." Emma looked at Greta quizzically. "Greta? Your manners? Come and help me with pinning this for Mrs van den Berg please."

Greta walked slowly across the room. She mustered her best smile. "Why yes, I think I showed your husband the garden there." She turned to her mother. "That's right, isn't it?"

Rosemary van den Berg smiled. "I wouldn't have recognised you in your school uniform. You looked so much older that day."

"I'm lucky that Mum makes me such lovely clothes." Greta held the gown where her mother indicated and Emma's hands flew deftly over it, pinning. She looked at her daughter keenly as her customer turned her back to them once more. Greta was flushed and seemed unusually flustered, though she was being very helpful. Why was she so unsettled by Rosemary, or was it the mention of Albert?

"And are you doing sixth form this year, Greta?" Rosemary inclined her head slightly and spoke over her shoulder.

Greta realised that she wasn't ugly, as she had remembered, or convinced herself. She was good looking, in an old woman sort of way. But her figure definitely was too heavy. Buxom, that was the word. She laughed inwardly, and it steadied her. "No, I will be next year."

"And then on to university?" Rosemary's voice carried a hint of superiority and scepticism.

"Most likely. I don't think Greta has really decided. My older girl is training to be a teacher." Emma spoke quietly. She would brook none of this. No one who entered her home got away with speaking down to her girls.

Greta felt something new and odd; she was grateful to her mother, for having the ability to put this woman in her place, for standing up for her with her rival. Albeit that her mother knew nothing of this fact and would have been mortified had she the slightest notion. She could see herself packed off to some distant relative in Jaffna or Trincomalee, as her mother did not have the finances to send her overseas. Such things did happen. Girls at school were ever ready to name the latest scandal and often seemed to be waiting eagerly for the next one.

Greta excused herself as soon as she could and hurried to her room. She shut the door and put a chair against it. She undid her tie and pulled her school uniform over her head, tossing both on the bed. She took off her school shoes and socks, and loosened her hair, shaking it free so it fell in a cascade of undulating waves around her face and down her back. She stood in front of the mirror in her underwear. She could see that her body was beautiful, perfect really, if she compared it to the images in magazines or the centuries old paintings of courtesans on a platform halfway up the rock fortress of Sigiriya.

She had climbed the rock on a holiday last Christmas with Miriam de Vos and her family. Miriam's very annoying older brother Arthur had pleaded with her to stand in front of the paintings, so he could take her photograph there, before his parents caught up with them. She'd had a surge of the devil and almost asked him if he wanted her to be bare breasted too, like the women in the paintings, but had fortunately resisted the urge as his parents got there just as he took the snap. They were odd with her for the rest of the trip anyway. Not at all fair, and not something she felt she could discuss with Miriam, who had raced on ahead to be the first to reach the top.

She felt a gush of triumph as she thought of the older woman in her mother's front room. How would Albert feel if she ever let him see her this way? She stared at her reflection, turning slowly from a frontal to a side view, then to the front again and to the other side for comparison. Finally, she turned her back to the mirror and looked over her shoulder. She smiled with satisfaction. But she needed to buy some women's underwear—a fancy bra and knickers—if she was seriously contemplating such a thing. It would not do to be seen in schoolgirl cotton.

* * *

"Ernest will be here any moment. Can't you send her out on an errand or something? She's so glum and rude to him. Lord knows he racks his brain to make conversation with her, and all he gets are monosyllables back!" Cynthia was pacing up and down the kitchen. She had an exam on Monday and this was the only time she would have with Ernest all weekend. She did not want Greta spoiling it.

Emma's tone was steady. "This is your sister's home too, darling. He'll just have to get used to it. I'm sure she's trying her best. Sixteen is an awkward age."

Emma had seen instantly that Ernest was attracted to Greta, it was very evident in the way he looked at her, though he seemed quite unaware of it himself; a common enough thing, especially with the young. It was also obvious that Greta could feel his attraction to her and it annoyed her, so she avoided him. Cynthia too must see the attraction, even if she denied it. It made things between the two sisters all the worse. Emma looked at her older daughter fondly. Cynthia was lovely, but Greta was stunning. There was no denying the fact that every male they met seemed to think so.

"That's rubbish, Mum. You've seen her after church. She can charm anyone she wants to, of any age, male or female! She's just like Dad!" This was a favourite ploy and a sure way of turning her mother against her sister: state the obvious and exaggerate it. Greta undoubtedly resembled their father more than she did, but they both had features from each of their parents. For some reason people always wanted to play up the differences between them. Cynthia had learned to make the most of it.

"That's quite enough, Cynthia! Why don't you go and call your sister to help set the table? Isn't Ernest going to be here any minute?" It was too blatant a move on this occasion. It irritated Emma and made her wonder how often she had been manipulated in this way. Although it was true that they would all have a far more pleasant afternoon, and the courtship between these two might progress far better without Greta in the house.

Cynthia reached her sister's door and knocked loudly. "Come and set the table! Ernest is coming for lunch."

"Do it yourself! I'm not your servant and I'm not waiting on your lover boy!" Greta shouted back through the closed door. Cynthia had been bossing her around all her life and she was sick of it. In fact, she was not going to follow Cynthia's orders anymore.

"You are the rudest creature I know! No one talks the way you do!"

Greta remained silent, and Cynthia became increasingly enraged. Greta's defiance of her had been growing steadily, but she had chosen this vitally important day to make some stupid stand. She was heartless and inconsiderate. She banged loudly on the door again. "Do as I say, Greta, or don't bother joining us for lunch." There was still no response from Greta. Cynthia stood at her sister's door and shouted. "I'll be so glad when we don't have to live together!"

"That makes two of us! Shall I tell Ernie to hurry and pop the question?"

Cynthia hated Greta at that moment. She hated how disrespectful Greta could be, how angry she could make her with just a few words. She wished they could send her away somewhere and have a peaceful home. But maybe she would have to be the one to leave? Maybe Greta was right. Perhaps she could leave with Ernest, sooner rather than later. This thought really appealed to her. He was an only child, and had no annoying siblings to contend with. But his mother was a widow too, and sickly and dependant on him, not such an attractive proposition. Still, he had a big house with far more room than this one, and three servants. They could not move out on their own. He certainly couldn't support her at this stage in his work as a junior accountant and she wouldn't be teaching for two years at least. Too long to wait for him, and to continue living with Greta.

Emma headed for the kitchen and smiled at Elly who had finished the cooking that morning and was about to leave for her afternoon off. "Everything ready, Madam." Elly nodded in the direction of the stove, where an array of saucepans stood with their lids on, then waved her hand at two dishes on a bench, each covered with a checked tea-towel. "The rice and pappadams."

"Thank you, Elly. I thought I'd be frying those myself." Emma smiled at the servant girl who was in her early twenties and always concerned, helpful, eager to please.

"You always busy, busy, Madam. You must rest, get young Missy to help." She worried about the mistress, she looked so old, so tired. Emma sighed deeply, and Elly looked at her quizzically.

Emma did her best to give her a reassuring smile. "Don't worry Elly. Go, enjoy yourself with your family. We'll manage lunch." How wonderful it would be if Greta had the slightest concern for her.

Greta felt hungry. She decided there was no reason she should be confined to her room because of Cynthia's foul mood and overanxiety about Ernest. She entered the kitchen and lifted the cloth covering the dish of pappadams, looking at her mother for permission.

"Just one, you know how Ernest loves them." Emma was searching through her kitchen cupboards, choosing appropriate serving dishes for the meal.

"No, truthfully, I had no idea." Greta's tone was mocking. She stared at her mother. "Does our world really have to revolve around Ernest?" Then she remembered that she wanted her mother to sew her a pleated red skirt, like the one she had seen in a magazine that morning, in time for Tuesday. No point getting off to a bad start. This meal was going to be an ordeal of its own making. "Okay, Mum, I'll be on my best behaviour. I always am when Ernest is around, but no one notices."

Emma stopped what she was doing and looked at her younger daughter, surprised by her attempt at conciliation. "I have noticed, Greta, and I know it can't be easy."

Greta paled slightly. Surely her mother could not be implying that she was attracted to that dullard Ernest, and struggling with it, insufferable! Nothing was further from the truth. It was simply too insulting. "He's not my type." Her voice was icy.

"I know that. It's not what I meant." Emma faltered. How could she speak plainly with Greta about the fact that she saw Ernest's attraction to her, and how awkward it made things for everyone, without hurting or insulting Cynthia? "You go set the table and I'll put on a cup of tea before he gets here. You haven't had breakfast, have you?"

Greta looked at her mother, surprised by the softness in her voice. She did not reply but turned and did as she asked.

Cynthia could not hear what they were saying but she heard the ebb and flow of conversation, then the friendly tone in her mother's voice. She should be pleased, Ernest often came early, might appear at any moment. It was good that there was no commotion or argument to greet him. But all she felt was jealousy. She was about to head into the kitchen, to set things right, remind her mother and her sister of her rightful place as the favoured daughter, when the doorbell rang. She changed direction and headed to the front door instead.

She opened the door to find Ernest on the front porch. He smiled at her somewhat shyly and held out a bunch of white lilies rimmed with palest pink. He looked flushed and a little awkward, but very pleased to see her. Her sister's mocking gibes rang in her ears: "your lover boy", "Shall I tell Ernie to hurry and pop the question?" Cynthia reached for the flowers, then cradled them lightly. She smiled slowly at Ernest. He lent forward and kissed her softly on the cheek. She shifted her head slightly and he took the invitation, kissing her gently on the lips. It was their first kiss; brief, tender. It marked a change in their relating.

Cynthia grasped his hand and led him into the front room. Her mother's dressmaking table with her sewing machine, measuring and marking tapes, patterns and pins, was confined to one side of the room and magically hidden behind their beautiful decorative screen. What remained was a warm and inviting space with two couches and a dining table.

Emma might not be financially flush, and their home might be rented, but her eye for beauty and flair for aesthetics extended well beyond her craft of dressmaking.

It had taken her some time after leaving Jürgen to really be able to establish her own home. She had found great pleasure in creating a place of beauty in which she and her daughters could live. This, together with founding a small but thriving business of her own and being able to support them all, had helped restore her sense of dignity, had eased some of the shame that had followed her father's death with its attendant loss of wealth and status. She was even, slowly but perceivably, finding some relief from the degradation that she had experienced in her marriage to Jürgen and its impact on her self-esteem.

Cynthia was proud of her mother and loved everything about the home that she had created for them, save Greta's presence in it. For Greta, life was far more complicated. Anything she might grudgingly admire about her mother felt like a betrayal of her father, whom she continued to love passionately, with the heart of a young child who has never had such love tested or tempered by reality.

"Please take a seat, Ernest. I'll just put these in water." Cynthia led him to the smaller of the two couches and waited until he was seated before releasing his hand and heading off still cradling the lilies he had given her. She was thrilled that he had kissed her. He had been both immensely surprised and pleased at this fortunate turn of events and the sudden progress in their relating. But seated in the drawing room and watching her retreat to the kitchen he felt more awkward and self-critical than ever. He was behaving like a trained dog. Why must he always struggle to be himself when he came to visit Cynthia in her home? He seemed to manage far better once they left its confines, albeit for a simple walk in the neighbourhood park and certainly on the rare occasions when they had gone to the pictures together on their own.

He felt lucky to have met Cynthia at all, as this had happened after a church service and it seemed that Cynthia's mother was not very religious. Her family only attended church at Easter and Christmas. He supposed he was also fortunate that they were allowed out on their own. Cynthia was only nineteen. Her mother did not seem to know that it was far more usual to send a younger sibling along with a courting couple. He really liked Greta, she was a very pretty girl who seemed shy and reserved, and rarely came out of her room. He felt sorry for her and even a little protective. But he was also pleased that Greta had never been made to accompany them, as this would have made things difficult and spoiled the happy experience of being able to walk and talk and hold hands with Cynthia in the park and at the cinema, all of which he loved. Besides, it was clear that Cynthia did not really like her younger sister, although he couldn't quite understand why.

"He's here early." Cynthia spoke softly and looked at her mother imploringly as she arranged the flowers in a long glass vase. "I'd just like a little time alone with him."

"Of course, darling, we'll come in with you now and say a quick hello, then leave the two of you alone until it's time for lunch."

"Just you, Mum, not her!" Cynthia looked up and glared at her sister.

"And which of us is still at school?" Greta turned toward the sink, taking her time to wash her tea cup. Her face was drawn. She was so tired of her sister's jibes. She couldn't help it that Ernest stared at her. She disliked the fact. Though she found she couldn't dislike Ernest completely, much as she enjoyed taunting Cynthia about him. He seemed good natured and quite unaware that he was staring at her like some overgrown boy. Oh, if only she was free to tell them about Albert: she had a real man who was in love with her! But Cynthia would never understand. It would be yet another reason to disapprove of her. Greta felt her chest tighten. Life in this house was so hard. She composed her face and looked at her mother. "Let's go and greet Ernest, Mum, then I'll help you warm up the lunch and serve." She turned to her sister. "Satisfied?"

But nothing Greta did or said could ever appease Cynthia. The year which Greta had spent with Inez and Edward had left Cynthia alone with her mother, at a time when Emma needed her daughter's love to sustain both her courage and sense of hope. They had visited Greta weekly and she had come to stay for a few weekends. But Cynthia had secretly hoped that Greta would be adopted, would no longer be relevant in their life. She was furious when her mother had refused this option and insisted her sister be returned to them as soon as Greta started school.

Most of all Cynthia loathed her younger sister for reminding her of a father she sought to drive from her memory, for retaining affection for him. Neither of them had coped with his sudden estrangement from them, let alone the news of his death less than two years later. Greta clung to her memory of him and longed that he might have lived to save her from the unhappiness of her life. Cynthia blamed him for the unhappiness in hers and strove to obliterate any tenderness she harboured for him. Both struggled with knowing how to love a real man.

The lunch was an awkward affair; Emma did her best to make conversation, Greta remained mute throughout; Cynthia was clearly furious and unable to contain her rage at her sister, however this impacted on an occasion that carried most significance for her. Ernest was convinced that the disharmony must somehow be his doing. But he was at a loss to know how to rectify it. Fortunately, the food was delicious, so after a significant period of sustained silent eating the courting couple excused themselves and left for a walk.

When they returned two hours later Emma opened the door and saw a Cynthia she barely recognised. Her daughter looked happier and more at peace than Emma could remember seeing her for years, maybe ever.

"Mrs de Zylva, may I have a word with you in private please?"

"Of course, Ernest." It could mean only one thing. Emma felt a sudden jolt of anxiety. She ushered Ernest into the drawing room and closed the doors at either end of the room. Cynthia hovered in the hallway for a few moments, then headed for the kitchen. Fortunately, Greta was nowhere about. She must be in her bedroom. Cynthia paced about in the kitchen. Surely her mother would say yes. Still, how was she going to settle herself and study for her exam? How could this be happening?

Ernest sat opposite Emma. He felt strangely confident. He had asked Cynthia, the girl he loved, to marry him, and she had said yes. His world had changed in a few short hours. He had become a man in his own eyes and in the eyes of his society. He had a fiancée. His mother would have to respect his need for his own life now, even if they lived with her. Cynthia wanted to get married as soon as they could. She had told him how much she longed to be with him. He had been too afraid to hope for such a thing, yet it was all true. From first kiss to engagement in a few short hours. But that was the way life happened sometimes. He knew about this. His own parents had met on holiday in Jaffna and become engaged within a week of that meeting. "I want to ask you for Cynthia's hand in marriage, Mrs de Zylva."

Emma remained silent. She looked very pale. She had not imagined losing one of her daughters at such a young age. Ernest began to feel nervous. It had not occurred to him she might say no, until this point. He suddenly remembered that she was a divorced woman, who was rumoured to have had a difficult marriage. He rose to his feet and stood in the space between the two couches. "I love Cynthia, Mrs de Zylva. She has said yes. You have my word, I will do everything I know to make her happy, to be a good husband to her, and a good father to our children."

Emma sighed, she could not stop this. She had no right to. It was what Cynthia wanted. She looked at Ernest and smiled gently. She needed to make him welcome. "I know you will, Ernest. I trust you to look after her and I know that you love her." She hesitated slightly. "I'm sure you'll be very happy together. Congratulations."

Ernest felt relief in every fibre of his body. Despite her words she seemed sad rather than happy, but she was losing her daughter. She must know they could not live in this small house with her. He moved towards her and bent to kiss her awkwardly on the cheek, then headed for the door. "I'll let Cynthia know." He rushed from the room.

Emma stared at the door waiting for Cynthia to burst through, preparing herself to be enthusiastic and full of congratulations for her daughter, who was so eager to rush into adult life. She remembered this strange stage of life so well; the hurry to have one's own say, to do it differently. She hoped more than anything that this would be the case for Cynthia, that she would never suffer the disappointments she had suffered in her own life. She remembered how her father's death had made marrying Jürgen so very urgent for her, how she had felt impelled to act, she'd had no room for thought. She had certainly suffered the consequences of her rash action. It was inconceivable that this would happen to Cynthia: Ernest was a kind and caring man, completely different to Jürgen, and yes, part of what she had told him was true. She believed that he loved Cynthia and would do his utmost to care for her. She hoped that the rest of it would come to pass. But how could anyone guarantee happiness?

* * *

Greta found it increasingly hard to focus on her schoolwork. It was the final class before school ended for the day. She was sweating profusely. It was not hotter than any other day, and she usually hardly perspired at all. She was just so excited and worried and nervous. Mrs Fonsake was reading out loud; a passage from Shakespeare's *A Midsummer Night's Dream*. At any moment she might ask them to read around the class. Greta hoped not. She didn't know if she could hold her nerve and not break into hysterical laughter or start crying. She had never done either of these things. But anything was possible today. Wasn't it? Wasn't that what she was thinking of, hoping for?

Titania and Bottom, was she being played for a fool, running to him this way? No, that was what Cynthia might call her, maybe her mother too? Strangely, she felt her mother might be more worried than angry, if she knew. But how could that be? Her mother didn't really care about her, never had. Anyway, her mother must never find out. This was her secret, something just for her. No one else must know. He had said so and she agreed. It made it all the more exciting, special. If Albert divorced his fat old wife and asked her to marry him, then she would let them all know. She wouldn't have to listen to Cynthia and her crowing about being engaged, and planning her silly wedding. It had only been three days since they'd got engaged and Cynthia was obsessed with the details of her wedding already. Of course, she had not been asked to be bridesmaid. That questionable honour was going to Cynthia's best friend Sylvia.

The class finally ended. She waited until most of the other girls got up from their desks and filed out. She walked slowly towards the door hoping not to catch anyone's eye.

"Greta, walk home with me? It's so hot. We can get an ice cream on the way. Never know we might run into some Peterites!"

"I can't, Miriam, I have to go to the dentist, in the Fort."

"That's a shame. My Mum has gone to stay with her sister in Negombo for a couple of days. I was hoping you'd come over and we could do our homework together, if we had no luck that is!" Miriam winked at her.

"Why don't we go to your place anyway and I can change there? I'll pick my bag up on the way home from the dentist. We can have that ice cream this Friday?" Greta laughed in a conspiratorial way. What a joke, playing at being excited about meeting schoolboys! But this was her chance. Miriam lived really close to school and her nosy disapproving mother was away. She had thought she'd have to change in the school toilets. But changing at Miriam's was a far better idea.

She was so excited about her outfit. Her mother had whipped her up the most beautiful red box-pleat skirt in heavy cotton, complete with satin lining. She had simply asked and here it was two days later. It was exactly what she wanted and most likely her compensation for Cynthia's appalling behaviour. In fact, she was sure of it. Her mother had a strange sense of fairness or guilt, or both, that motivated her at times of conflict and change. She did not understand it, but it was sometimes turned to her advantage. She had rolled the skirt carefully to keep the pleats crisp. She had a lovely lightweight blouse, white with little black polka dots, and sandals to complete the outfit. She repacked her school bag, with her body shield-ing what she was doing, as she removed her treasured outfit, placed her books at the bottom of the bag and her clothes back on top, careful so as not to crush them.

* * *

"Greta, you look so beautiful!" Miriam eyed her friend in admiration. Then her expression changed. "But eye makeup and lipstick? For the dentist?"

"Who else?"

"Arthur will be home at any minute." Miriam seemed genu-inely worried.

Greta burst out laughing. It really was too much! Arthur! Why did everyone think she was attracted to their boring brothers and boyfriends, when they were the ones who couldn't take their stupid eyes off her? For weeks now she'd had a wonderful man who adored her and who she longed to be with. It just wasn't fair that she couldn't tell them all. She felt sorely tempted to tell Miriam, if only to dispel the insult and quell her sense of injustice. But she stopped herself. He had said to tell no one. "Miriam, you're the one who asked me here, remember? I was going to change at school."

* * *

She hurried into Carghills, past the rows of dresses and tops in ladies' wear, heading for the lingerie department in the most confident manner she could muster. But her heart was racing. She knew she did not look like a schoolgirl in this outfit. She could pass for twenty at least, but she felt jittery inside, like a criminal. She had after all stolen the money for this purchase from her mother, or rather topped up her own savings. She had no idea what a fancy bra and knickers might cost. Her mother had always come with her for any such purchases and had steered her to the appropriate racks. She would pay her mother back, if she did need to dip into that extra money, as soon as she got some money for her birthday, probably from Inez and Edward. She felt a sudden surge of revulsion at the idea of those two funding her sexy underwear.

She stopped abruptly. There were two whole racks of beautiful underwear directly in front of her. Such gorgeous things. What colour should she choose; red to match her skirt? But something in her knew that was not quite right. She lifted a pair of powder-blue satin panties from one rack and found a matching bra in her size on the next. She headed for the fitting rooms. She noticed that her hand was trembling, ever so slightly, as she gripped her chosen items firmly.

"In here, Miss." The shop girl smiled at her and held the curtain to the cubicle open.

She did her best to appear calm and self-assured. She smiled as the curtain fell behind her.

"Just call out if you need a hand with the hooks or any change of size."

"Yes, yes, thank you, I will." She tugged at the curtain making certain it was fully closed. She was quivering with anticipation and fear. But she needed to do this. She was committed now.

* * *

Greta looked up at the office building on the opposite side of the street. He had told her that his office was on the first floor. Did it face the street? Could he see her now? Would he recognise her, dressed as she was, looking so much older, more sophisticated? His wife had said she looked older the day they all met at Inez's house. But she knew that the dress she had worn that day was nothing compared to this outfit. She felt glamorous, that was it. Maybe it was due to the underwear she was wearing, maybe it was the skirt, or perhaps it was due

95

to her sense of excitement and adventure at doing something utterly daring in coming here to meet him.

She saw a phone box fifty metres away. What luck, there were so few about. She hurried there and entered it. She closed the door and searched in her little black handbag for the coins that she had tossed in for exactly this purpose. She dialled and listened to the droning noise of the phone ringing repeatedly at the other end. "Hello, Mr van den Berg's office." His secretary had a sing-song voice.

Greta wondered how old she was. "Hello, this is Miss de Zylva for Mr van den Berg. He's expecting my call."

"Just a moment, Miss de Zylva. I'll put you through."

"Miss de Zylva!" Albert laughed loudly. "Where are you, beautiful? I thought we had a rendezvous scheduled this afternoon?"

Greta loved the sound of his voice, his easy assurance. It made her feel like she could do anything, like everything in life would be okay, as long as she could be with him. "We do, I'm just down the road from your office, in a phone box."

He laughed again. "You are resourceful! But no need for the cloak and dagger theatrics, much as I'm enjoying them. Just come on up to my office. My secretary will show you in."

Greta felt a little disappointed and somewhere a vague sense of alarm began to stir. Was his secretary so used to showing young women into his office? No, surely, he must have made out that she was a business associate of his. But this was hard for her to justify, even in her heightened state of excitement and anticipation. Did men in their forties really have female business associates in their teens, even if they were dressed to impress and happened to look twenty years old on the day? She decided not to dwell on the subject. He was in the building across the street and he was expecting her. It was all that mattered.

She crossed the street and entered his office building. She slowed her pace as she climbed the stairs to the first floor, trying to steady herself. Her pulse was racing. She stood outside his office and stared at the logo embossed in gold letters on the upper glass panel of the door in front of her—"Van Den Berg Enterprises". She reached out, grasped the doorknob and turned it. She was in a small rectangular anteroom; a few wooden chairs lined one wall, a table strewn with magazines stood alongside them. His secretary was seated at a desk in front of her.

The rapid metallic clanging of typewriter keys ceased abruptly. His secretary looked up and smiled. Greta noticed how white her teeth looked against her dark skin, and that her smile seemed genuine. She was in her early thirties, Sinhalese and dressed in a smart blouse and skirt. "Miss de Zylva?"

Greta nodded.

"Mr van den Berg is expecting you. Go straight in. You're lucky, he's just finished for the day. I'm sure he'll get you to your concert in time." She nodded at a wooden door and began typing again.

Her English was excellent. Greta was mildly surprised. It seemed that he had passed her off as a relative, or the daughter of a friend he was doing a favour for. There was not the slightest hint that his secretary thought anything was amiss. This must mean he was not a lecher, surely? Greta rapped lightly on the door and opened it. He was sitting, pen in hand, at a large mahogany desk cluttered with papers. A small window beside his desk looked out over the alleyway between this office block and the next. He sat back and looked at her as she gently pressed her back against the door behind her to close it, then stood there leaning against it. "Don't you look a picture." He stared at her hard. He put his pen down and stood, reaching out casually to close the blind on the window, then taking his seat again. "Come here." His voice was smooth, commanding.

Greta felt aroused in a way she never had before. Her body tingled. Her belly ached. She knew she had to obey him, whatever he wanted of her. She walked around the desk and stood in front of him. He looked her up and down smiling all the time. He reached for her hand and took it, pulling her around to sit on his lap. She felt his penis hard against her bottom as he fondled her breasts and kissed the back of her neck. Suddenly his hand was inside her panties rubbing against her in some way that felt amazing, then his fingers were inside her. "Come, my little beauty, I'm going to give you exactly what you're asking for." His mouth was next to her ear, whispering hoarsely, then licking her neck. Greta looked towards the door. He laughed. "Don't worry she won't suspect a thing. She'll ring first if she needs me."

Greta's mind was racing. He talked about his secretary as if she were some loyal trained dog who did his unquestioned bidding. Her heart began to pound more than ever. She felt frightened now, as well as aroused, but ultimately compelled to do whatever he asked of her. He stood and held her tight against him, her back still against him. He lifted her skirt and laughed softly once more when he saw her pale blue underwear. "For me? How lovely!" She registered the half-mocking tone of his voice. He dragged her new panties down her legs. She kicked off her sandals and kicked the silky garments away from her. His hands were up under her blouse suddenly, fondling her breasts, undoing her bra, undoing his trousers which fell to the ground along with his underwear. He rubbed his erect penis against her bottom. He turned her sharply around and began sucking at her right nipple. A jolt of intense pleasure and pain shot through her body. He spun her around once more and bent her over the desk. His fingers were inside her vagina, no her anus, no both.

"So wet, so luscious, so delicious." He was whispering into her ear as he lent over her. He was biting her neck. She shuddered and gave a small cry as his penis entered her vagina and thrust hard inside her. He put his hand over her mouth. "Shush, shush little Greta. This is our secret." His thrusting was harder and harder. Waves of pleasure and pain kept hitting her body. She couldn't tell what was happening. Then he wasn't there anymore and then he was poking at her anus, poking and thrusting hard. "Come on, little girl, you know you want me."

She tried to say something, but his hand tightened over her mouth. "No noise!" His voice was sharp, commanding. "Pretend you're going to the toilet, open your bottom! Now! … that's right, that's lovely, lovely, that's my girl, lovely." Her bottom was on fire, everything ached and burnt. She wanted to scream, she wanted to cry. She didn't want him to be angry. She didn't want him to blame her, to hate her. Finally, he stopped it. He sighed deeply and lay his head against her back. He pulled his penis out of her. He laughed a strange rasping laugh as he wiped himself with some tissues from a box on his desk. He handed a wad of them to her. She looked up at him blankly, dazed. "Go on, take them. Wipe yourself and get dressed." She did as he said. "Come on, we'd better get going." He looked at her oddly, and smiled. "Well? Was that what you wanted?"

* * *

Greta stared in the mirror. She looked as scared as she felt. Her period was two weeks late. It used to come late or early sometimes when she first got it at thirteen, but it had been very regular for the last two years. Could she be pregnant? Could you get pregnant if someone had sex with your bottom? She didn't think so. But then he didn't always finish up in her bottom, just most of the time. He'd been picking her up on the way back from school at least once a week, sometimes twice, once even three times. He drove her to a house he had, not too far away from where she lived. She didn't know where exactly. They always drove up the driveway and went in through the back door. It was a fully furnished house, but the owners must be away overseas or something.

Maybe some friends of his owned it. He treated the place as if he owned it. He didn't care much about the owners, if they were friends. He made her take her clothes off as soon as they walked inside. They had sex everywhere; in the lounge room, in the kitchen, on the floor, but almost never in the bedroom. Once he even took her outside naked to a shaded corner of the garden and made her bend over on the back lawn. He kept his own clothes on that time. It made her feel awful, like she was an animal or something, but he'd got more excited than ever, had really hurt her with his thrusting.

She knew somehow that he didn't care much about her. Not when he ordered her around the way he did. Yet, somewhere else inside her, she believed that he loved her, that he was going to leave his wife some day and marry her. But a niggling voice kept asking the pressing question; did someone treat their wife the way he treated her? She couldn't imagine Ernest doing these things Albert did to her to Cynthia, or making Cynthia do the things Albert made her do.

Could she be pregnant? He most often ejaculated in her bottom or in her mouth. She was pretty sure that he had to ejaculate in her vagina to make a baby. But he had done that once or twice. Not very often, if she thought about all the times they'd had sex. But she had heard someone at school talking about a girl who got pregnant after having sex only one time. That seemed terribly bad luck.

What was she going to do? If she was pregnant she only had a short time when she could have an abortion, after that it was supposed to be too dangerous. That's what they all said. Millicent Loos was rumoured to have had an aunt who died that way. Just the rumour affected Millicent's reputation as well. Made her seem tainted. What would happen to her reputation if anyone found out? It was bad enough that her parents were divorced. It was somehow even shameful that her father was dead. Maybe she could ring Albert and let him know. Maybe he would leave his wife now and marry her and she could have the baby. She was suddenly frightened to tell him. What if he got angry? He did awful things to her even when he wasn't angry. He thought what he was doing to her was funny; he would laugh if she let him see that he was really hurting her and go all the harder. So, she did her best not to show him. She'd tell him over the phone.

* * *

The phone rang once, twice, he picked up. "What are you doing calling me here?" He sounded annoyed, but then he softened. His voice was silky. "It's okay as it turns out, my wife is out. Would you like me to come and pick you up, my delicious little bit of cunt?" He had started calling her this whenever they spoke alone. She dared not ask anyone what it meant and it never occurred to her to look in the dictionary. "I'd be oh so happy to give you what you can't get enough of. What do you say, meet me in half an hour at the corner of Dickmans Road?"

"No, Albert, no, I can't." Her voice was trembling, she blurted it out. "I think I'm pregnant."

"You stupid little slut! Well, you're on your own with it. If you tell anyone it's me, I'll deny it. Had to spoil things, didn't you?"

"Albert, you said we'd get married someday. You said you love me."

"I am married, my gullible little missy! And if I was free, do you really think I'd marry someone as cheap as you?"

She let the phone drop and hang dangling from its cord as she pulled the door of the phone booth open. She ran down the street. Her head was spinning. She couldn't think. A horn beeped loudly. She had run across the next road without looking. She stood on the kerb and turned to face the stream of traffic that had started when the light changed at the intersection a few hundred metres up the road. She thought about stepping into the traffic. She stood still and shook her head slowly from side to side trying to clear it. What was she going to do?

* * *

She was bleeding so heavily. Something had gone wrong with the operation. Maybe she was going to die. Albert had found her a place to have it done, had given her the money after all. Maybe he had been afraid she'd have the baby. But she'd had to go to that terrible place on her own. She didn't want to think about it. She felt so cold, she began to tremble. She was moaning with pain. There was a knock on the door.

"Greta? Greta, are you alright? … I'm coming in." The door opened and Emma saw her daughter curled up on the bed, ghostly white. "What's the matter, Greta?" But somewhere she knew, sensed the bleeding, deadly bleeding. This was how she must have looked after Greta's birth and the haemorrhage that followed.

Greta remained silent. She had to tell her mother. She couldn't find the words.

"Are you having a miscarriage?" Emma's voice was calm.

She'd always suspected that her mother just wanted her dead, but she sounded terribly worried, not angry. "No, I had an abortion."

"Who? …"

"I don't know, I just went to the place, I can't even remember where it was, it was so awful …" She began to sob, deep wracking sobs.

"Who is the father? Albert van den Berg?"

She knew! How did she know?

Emma snapped. "If your father was here he'd kill him!" Her voice was steely, full of rage and grief. Had this happened because she had left Jürgen?

"But my father is dead!!!" Greta was shrieking. Someone was rapping on the door. Her mother opened the door, then went out of the room shutting it behind her. She could hear Cynthia outside. "If anyone finds out, if this ruins things for Ernest and me, I'll never forgive her! I hate her, the horrid little slut, I hate her!"

CHAPTER FIVE

Colombo, Friday 25th September 1964

Jeff rounded the corner into his street. He cruised quietly below the overhanging branches of the flamboyant trees. It had been such a challenging day and there was surely more to come. The late afternoon sun shot sudden glancing rays through the canopy above him. He pulled over and let his car idle quietly for a moment. This had been his street for most of his life. The house where he and Greta lived had belonged to his parents, been his home since he was a young child. He realised that he loved the beauty of this street; its stillness, the trees lining it that filtered the light through their dense green foliage and coral coloured blooms, the large elegant houses amid their lush, spacious gardens. He saw it all anew, as he understood that he was leaving.

Maybe he could put this off another day, talk to Greta over the weekend, go to the party tonight and simply enjoy himself. Yet, he knew he could not. He had told others, he must tell her, take her with him, somehow. He had asked Kingsley to help, and he might oblige, though his surprisingly intense reaction to the news that they were leaving no longer made it a sure thing. He couldn't count on Kingsley's backing. A startling fact. Impossible to imagine only a day ago. Nothing was a given. He baulked at the thought, the reality of it. But the thing was in motion, and he had to see it through. He sighed as he took his foot off the brake and placed it lightly on the accelerator. The car moved forward once more. He turned the wheel and let it roll gently in through the gates and onto the circular drive, stopping at last at his front porch.

Greta had appeared suddenly in the back drawing room and began pacing back and forth in front of her mother. "You couldn't let it go, could you? Cynthia, and how hard life is for her! Cynthia!"

Sylvia and Johann had left an hour earlier, and Leila had gone to find Charlotte and play in the garden while her mother and grandmother rested. Emma had been reading quietly and waiting for Jeff, who gave her a ride home after most of her visits, or at least to her bus stop, as he would today.

She was alarmed by her daughter's sudden reappearance and tirade. "Greta, what is it? I don't understand what's got into you. You had a pleasant lunch with Sylvia, surely? Your dress is beautiful. You and Jeff are going out tonight. What is the matter? Are you pregnant again?"

Greta sneered at her mother wordlessly then marched to the window, turned her back to her and looked out. She felt on the verge of screaming. She had no idea why she'd been so on edge all day. She just felt intensely irritated by everyone. "No, I'm not pregnant! But I meant what I said before, why don't you go and live with Cynthia and Ernest in England? She'd love to have you there!"

Emma's voice was steady. "I know she would. The truth of it is that I've been waiting to see what you and Jeff are planning. None of us can afford to stay, given the choice."

Greta spun around instantly to stare at her mother. She recognised her mother's intelligence and knew that Emma was far better informed about current events than she was, or had any desire to be. Uncertainty and fear flittered across her face. Finally, she spoke, her voice hesitant. "You truly believe that?"

"Of course, I do! There are more race riots on the way, I have no doubt of it. The Sinhalese and Tamils have hated each other

104

for centuries. You've studied history. They were endlessly at war before the colonial era. The Sinhala nationalists have made it abundantly clear that Ceylon should be a Sinhalese nation. They are quite rabid!" Emma's voice was quiet and clear, there was a steely tone to it, filled with distaste.

"So, you're not just talking about loss of position in society? You think we're in actual physical danger here?" She was struggling to take it in, to fathom something that seemed so impossible to her.

Emma stared directly in front of her, contemplating a future that might bring the worst. She forced herself to speak the words she dreaded. "Civil war is what I fear most. This is no place for Leila."

"Leila!!" Greta almost shrieked the name.

Leila had been making her way slowly along the veranda. She wanted to see her grandmother and spend whatever time she could with her before she left to go back to her own home. Gran must have finished her rest by now. As she drew near the main house she heard her mother and her grandmother talking, and the intensity in their voices. She slipped down off the veranda in fear and began walking slowly through the garden instead. Suddenly her mother screamed her name. She didn't know what to do. Was she being summoned? Should she hurry to her mother, or turn and run back to the servants' quarters? The soft distant crunching of tyres on the gravel drive distracted her instantly. She bolted around the side of the house to jump into her father's arms as he climbed out of his car.

"Oh Daddy!" She sighed as she nuzzled against his neck. She felt safe at last.

He gave her a warm hug and a kiss, then placed her on the ground and took her hand. "How's my favourite girl?" He smiled as she looked up at him. "Or should I say my favourite little girl. Where's that gorgeous mother of yours?"

"I think Mummy's been fighting with Gran about something." She spoke softly and scuffed her feet in the gravel.

"Fighting?" Jeff van Buuren seemed bemused. "I'd be surprised, I'm sure Emma's too wise for that. We all know who'd win that battle!" His voice trailed off as he murmured to himself with the sense of a man who was starting to realise his own limitations. He smiled gently at Leila. "Don't mind me, poppet. Let's go and find them, shall we?"

They entered the back drawing room and Jeff let go of Leila's hand as Greta rushed to greet him. She swayed as his arm encircled her waist and he stooped to kiss her on her cheek. She began to play distractedly with the lapels of his jacket. "Thanks for making it home, darling. The Leembruggens are expecting us at seven. What an ungodly hour for a party! I think they're going to make some sort of announcement. But I'm pretty sure it's good news, something exciting. I asked Sylvia at lunch, she more or less confessed to it, though she'd been sworn to secrecy." Her tone was light, forced and unconvincing, her words spilling out rapidly. "I was so afraid they were going to announce that they're the next ones off to Australia!"

Before he could respond she turned to look at her mother, whether daring her to broach this dreaded topic once more or attempting to silence her it was impossible to tell. Instead she caught sight of Leila, who had hurried silently to her grandmother's side for safety and now stood beside her, her hand resting on her grandmother's knee. Greta's voice became an acid barb. "I think it's time you left, Mum. Jeff can drive you to your bus."

Jeff felt deeply shocked by Greta's strange behaviour, but he maintained his equilibrium as he gently disentangled himself from her embrace and moved forward to greet his mother-in-law. Emma's visits were a weekly occurrence. He knew that Greta was often brusque with her mother, but he could not remember such blatant rudeness in years. Not since she was pregnant. Her pregnancies had all been difficult. She had become irritable and sharp with everyone around her, except for him. He had been confused by the extreme calmness that then followed her two miscarriages and was distressed by her lack of affection for their baby daughter when she was born.

He had hoped that this would change with time, but it had not. Her inability to love Leila was the true reason he wanted no more children with her. He passed it off as the result of being an only child himself. In truth, neither of them wanted more children. He didn't know and had never asked Greta her reasons. But he was profoundly grateful for the love given his daughter by her ayah and her grandmother. It was some compensation.

He found himself mulling this over in the few seconds it took him to make his way across the room to greet Emma. Had the unexpected talk of Amy unsettled him? Was it the recognition that he feared talking to his wife directly about the most crucial things in life? He realised with surprise that there was so much they never spoke of. Yet, he and Amy had talked easily about everything. He corrected himself—until it came to the time of their parting. Then their conversations had been unexpected, jarring. The reality that one of them must leave their homeland so that they might be together had severed their relationship in a way he could not have imagined possible.

He leant forward and kissed Emma on the cheek. "How are you, Mrs de Zylva?"

"Well, thank you, Jeff, but a little tired." Emma felt weary at the thought of the day she had spent with Greta and her long bus trip home. Then she felt the warmth of her granddaughter's hand resting on her knee. She roused herself. She smiled affectionately as she looked from Leila to her father. "But we've had a fine time, haven't we?"

Leila looked up at her father, and tried to be cheerful and agree with Gran. "Yes." But her voice was hesitant, subdued. It had been a dreadful day really, Mummy had been acting so strangely to everyone and Charlotte was staying away from all of them.

"Damned by faint praise, Mum!" Greta laughed strangely and they all turned to look at her. Her expression was contemptuous, her smile more akin to a sneer, her beauty undone. She seemed pleased to be the focus of their attention once more.

Jeff looked at her evenly, but with an inward jolt. Did he blind himself to this side of her nature? How often did she behave this way without his registering the fact? "What about a drink, darling?" He turned from Greta to her mother. "Join me in a whisky, Mrs de Zylva, or a gin and tonic for the road?"

"A sherry would be lovely." Emma accepted Jeff's hospitality without looking at her daughter. He was attempting to force Greta to obey social norms, but Emma had no idea how Greta might respond today.

"Of course, of course." Greta left the room and hurried away to the sideboard in the dining room. She felt a deep sense of pride in her capacity to fulfil the role of wife and hostess. She did not for a moment comprehend that Jeff was upset by her behaviour and was attempting to defuse the situation and break the tension in the room. She seemed not to remember that this level of formality, offering her mother a drink, or Jeff having a drink as he came home, was completely out of their normal rhythm of relating, something Jeff might do only if Kingsley were to accompany him home in the evening, as he sometimes did. However, while pouring the drinks she thought at once of Kingsley and of the prospect of dancing with him at the party tonight. She smiled with pleasure. He was such an amazing dancer.

"Leila, where is Charlotte?" Jeff noted her absence as soon as Greta left. Charlotte would ordinarily be here by this time, aware that Emma was about to leave, helping Leila say goodbye, leading her away to have dinner in a quiet, seamless manner that left them all satisfied.

"I think she's staying away on purpose. Mummy's been horrid to her all day. She's probably sick of it." Leila looked at him intensely. It was more than she had ever said in direct criticism of her mother. She took her mother's mixed and unpredictable behaviour to her for granted. It was terrifying at times, but it was all she had ever known. She had seen her mother be rude to Gran occasionally in the past as well. But her mother had always been civil and matter of fact in her dealings with Charlotte. Leila hated the way her mother had behaved all day to the ayah that she loved. Perhaps Daddy could help. It was worth a try.

Before Jeff could respond Greta was back with a small silver tray. She served Jeff his tumbler of whisky first, then somewhat reluctantly offered the tray to her mother before taking the second sherry glass herself. She held her glass up. "To a wonderful evening."

They sipped at their drinks in silence. Jeff held his hand out to his daughter. "Come with me, Leila. Let's go see where Charlotte is, shall we?" He turned to Emma. "Excuse me for a moment? We won't be long."

Greta snorted. "Yes, Charlotte's been acting strangely and getting on my nerves! I don't know what's wrong with everyone today." Her annoyance increased. "It's time for Leila's dinner. Tell her to feed Leila and come and see me after."

"Don't worry about that, darling, I'll talk to Charlotte. Won't you need to get ready? What about showing me that new dress?" It dawned on Jeff with a jolt that he was placating her. It was so familiar. Might he do this all the time, without fully realising? He felt unnerved by this sudden recognition of the vapidity in his communication with his wife. When and how had it devolved to this?

He turned to his daughter. "Why don't you give Gran a kiss goodbye, Leila? You can stay with Charlotte and have your dinner when we find her." Leila immediately hugged her grandmother and they kissed fondly in parting. She took her father's hand and looked up at him as they walked out into the garden. She felt the hot moist air hit her face and peered through the fading light into the lush greenness of the garden.

She heard a magpie calling as it flew over them and landed in one of the larger trees. It was so lovely out here, walking with Daddy, going to find Charlotte. Maybe Daddy could sort this out with Mummy and they could go back to how it had been. Maybe Mummy would wake in a better mood, be different tomorrow. But this was the first time Charlotte had not come to get her for her dinner. Something was very wrong.

Charlotte had remained in the kitchen with Rani deliberately. She did not want to be spoken to rudely in front of the mistress's mother. She liked Mrs de Zylva and knew that she loved her granddaughter. She wanted to find a way to stay with Leila for as long as she could, but she would not be humiliated or shamed. She heard voices. It was Leila and the master. She could not remember ever seeing him down near the kitchens and servant quarters. She exchanged a look of surprise with Rani as she got to her feet and walked out of the kitchen door. The master and Leila were laughing together as they came into sight.

Leila ran to her side and caught her hand. "Charlotte, Charlotte, Daddy was just telling me about the tricks he used to play on the servant boy and cook when he was little. Right here, in our kitchen!"

Charlotte smiled. Of course, the master had grown up in this house. His ayah must have lived in the servants' quarters, perhaps even in her room. He would most certainly have played in the kitchen as a child, just as Leila did. This had never occurred to her before. But she rarely saw him. He was gone early in the morning and ate in the main house at night. She always saw him in the company of the mistress at bedtimes and at the weekends. All her instructions came from the mistress. It was the first time he had ever sought her out. She felt both a little shy and somewhat intimidated. Yet, she knew him to be a kind man in his dealings with everyone. She had been there in the background for the past four years, caring for Leila at home and whenever the family socialised with other families who had children. She genuinely liked the master and recognised that he liked her and was grateful for the care that she gave his child. She had often wondered how such a man could have married her mistress and had a child with her.

"Hello, Charlotte, I've brought Leila down to have dinner with you. She tells me it's been a difficult day?" He was looking at her calmly. He recognised her discomfort and glanced at her in passing before addressing his comments to the evening at large.

She was grateful. She had met his eyes for a moment before looking down. She said nothing. It was not her place to raise any issue she might have with her mistress.

"I told Daddy that Mummy's been awful to you today, Charlotte." The little girl's voice was so musical, yet filled with indignation.

Charlotte could barely grasp it. This beautiful child, who suffered her mother's abrasiveness, slights and sour temper with never a word of protest when turned her way, had complained to her father the instant it had impacted on her ayah. She was deeply touched and close to tears. Yet, she could never let this be seen by her master. She felt a sudden strange lightening within. She had worried about the little one for so long, that she had not the strength to withstand the life she must endure with her mother. Yet, perhaps after all, there was hope.

"Charlotte, can you tell me what's been going on? Has my wife insulted you?" Jeff imagined his own ayah, and how incensed she would have been if she had been treated rudely. A thing that would never have occurred in his parents' home, and so she had stayed as a house servant until they died. Charlotte remained silent. She could not bring herself to speak up against her mistress. But she recognised that she must somehow confirm what Leila was saying or else risk betraying the child. It would be confusing for Leila if she did not speak. It was not what she needed. Her mother was a strange and confusing person and Charlotte knew that Leila relied on her

111

directness and her no-nonsense view of life to help her make sense of the world.

"I think the mistress no want me here now." It was difficult but she had to go on. "Still, I would like to stay longer, if that can be so." Leila was listening, but it was better that she heard this now, from her, and understand that she did not want to go, than to find herself ordered to leave suddenly, or be compelled by the mistress's intolerable treatment to go, with no chance to say goodbye to the child.

Jeff reeled inwardly. Why today? He knew that this night he must find the time and courage, somehow, to talk to Greta about the necessity of leaving Ceylon. He wanted Charlotte to stay while they organised their departure, to care for Leila at a time of upheaval and change, to help her with the transition. She and Leila would have to part. It was inevitable. But his hope was that this could be handled well. The last thing Leila needed was Charlotte's premature departure. He needed her to stay until they left. He was not at all certain how Greta would react to his decision. "I would like you to stay, Charlotte. I will speak to my wife."

"Thank you, Sir." It was more than Charlotte had antici- pated or imagined she would hear from him.

Leila hugged Charlotte fiercely around her waist. "You see, Charlotte, you see. I knew Daddy would help!" It was not entirely true. Leila had long hoped that her father might be able to do something about the problem of Mummy. But she had never before dared test her hope or risk being disappointed by him. It had been such an odd day, with so many different things going on, some good, some bad. But the terrible fear that had come when her mother was so rude to Charlotte felt a little better.

"I'm going up to the main house now, Leila, to give Gran a lift to her bus stop." Jeff bent and kissed his daughter's head. He turned to Charlotte. "I'll be gone for half an hour or so."

112

The message was clear; stay here and away from any potential conflict until then. He walked slowly through the garden that he loved. The sun was low in the sky and the birds were noisily settling in to roost for the night. He stopped, stood for a moment, and felt the warmth of the air against his skin, then climbed the few steps onto the back veranda and entered the drawing room at the back of the house.

Emma was seated on a sofa reading a book. She looked up at him. A rapid glance that held both pain and quiet desperation passed between them, before either roused themselves enough to guard against such candour. A reprieve came with Greta's sudden entrance. She was there to show Jeff her new dress, and in truth, to get her mother's final approval. She stood in the doorway and turned from side to side. The bodice of the dress clung firmly, exposing just a hint of cleavage, the slender straps revealed the beauty of her shoulders and arms, while the full skirt swayed as she moved.

Jeff smiled at her with genuine pleasure. "You're a vision, darling! I think the rubies, don't you?"

Greta face glowed with pleasure. It was exactly what she had planned; her ruby necklace and earrings would be a perfect contrast with the emerald of the dress. She turned to her mother.

"You look lovely, Greta, he's done a marvellous job." There was no hint of resentment, hurt or competition in Emma's voice, though her daughter always listened for them.

Greta had refused to let her mother make any clothes for her from the day that she married. She had also refused to let her make clothes for her granddaughter. She was waiting for the day her mother would finally acknowledge the impact of this on her. She longed to provoke her mother into some reaction that would confirm that she had inflicted pain. But again today she had to content herself with the truth in her mother's compliment instead.

"We'd best leave, Mrs de Zylva. I don't like the thought of you walking far at night, but I'm afraid there's no time for me to drive you home."

Such a surprising comment. It took Emma off-guard. Jeff always drove her home when he could, but he had dropped her at her bus stop countless times before with good humour and no apparent concern. "That's kind of you, Jeff. But I'm very used to walking around on my own. I've been doing it for almost twenty-five years!"

Greta's mood had risen at the sight of herself in the mirror, the genuine compliments that had come her way and the thought of an evening where she would be admired by all who saw her. She walked forward and kissed her mother briefly in parting then stroked her husband's arm. "Hurry back?"

They drove in silence for most of the way. It was a short drive and Jeff had no intention of discussing his plans with his mother-in-law, not until he had convinced Greta first. But something felt compelling. Emma was a sensible, thoughtful woman who he suddenly suspected might have a better idea about the difficult side of Greta's personality than he did. He pulled the car over just short of her bus stop. The streets were alive with people, walking on their way home from work or on their way out to visit friends or to have dinner. He turned in his seat and looked at Emma.

"What is it, Jeff? Has something difficult happened?"

He laughed. "No, but it's about to. My friend Ronald de Souza has offered me a place in his legal firm in Melbourne." He shifted in his seat. "To be honest, I asked him if he'd have a place for me, and he has been very enthusiastic about the possibility of our settling there." He paused. "Do you know him, or his family? He left for Australia before Greta and I met."

"I know of his family. We never socialised, but by all accounts, they are lovely people, kind and well respected."

114

"Ronald has always been one of my closest friends. Well, he and Kingsley of course." He stared ahead then turned to look at her. "You don't seem surprised?"

"I was hoping you had begun to make plans, or think about your options at least. Greta and I were talking about it this afternoon."

He stared at her in amazement. He had a sudden urge to hug her but restrained himself.

"Yes, she suggested I go to England to be with Cynthia and her family. But I told her I was waiting to see what the two of you were planning. She seemed quite shocked when I mentioned the possibility of civil war."

"Oh, I hope it never comes to that!" He sat staring ahead silently, then spoke again, his tone sombre. "I suppose there is a very real possibility of things escalating that far. I've allowed myself the thought that we must get out before there are more riots. I really don't want to think about how much worse it could get." He sighed deeply. "Let's just hope that sanity prevails." He turned to look at her directly once more. "Would you consider coming with us, for both Greta and Leila's sake? Well maybe for all three of us." He laughed anxiously. "I'd understand, of course, if you want to go to England instead to be with Cynthia and your nephews." He was trying to be solicitous, but his tone of voice altered at the mention of Cynthia's name. He had no time for his sister-in-law, in fact he despised her. "Just think about it please."

Emma looked at him steadily. "I've already made up my mind, Jeff. I'm very grateful for your offer, and I will come, if Greta will allow it." Her tone became deadly serious. "Leila needs me."

He sighed deeply with relief. He could not take this conversation further. He needed all his emotional reserve to contend with Greta. He must now convince her to migrate to Australia and to take her mother with them. He needed to find a way for her to see it as a necessity. It would be the best option. He realised that Emma was still looking at him keenly. "Leave it to me. I'll find a way to convince her." She was about to open her door and leave when he placed his hand on her arm and stopped her. "Don't let her know about this conversation please. It will work far better if she believes that she's the one inviting you."

"So, you do know her." She smiled at him and left.

He did a slow U-turn in the crowded street, beeping his horn as he manoeuvred his way through the steady stream of pedestrians on either side of the road and began his drive home. If Emma came with them they had a far greater chance of a stable home life. He did not want to acknowledge that he was really asking his mother-in-law to do an ayah's job. But he recognised that Emma loved Leila in a way that Greta never could and he was sure that her even temper and common sense would help improve their chance of succeeding in a new and very different country. Ronald wrote in glowing terms of his life in Melbourne, but Ronald had married his childhood sweetheart, who was both sophisticated and kind.

Amy's face came suddenly to mind and he cursed quietly to himself. Why? Why now? Wasn't this day gruelling enough without being haunted by the memory of someone he had left behind years ago? Yet, she was someone for whom he had considered giving up his country and life as he then knew it. The issue of changing country and the challenges it had entailed for each of them had led to an ending; had brought further heartache at a time he was barely coping with the intense grief and loss of his parents' sudden death. Perhaps it made sense that she was playing on his mind this way, fuelling his sense of apprehension, after so many years in the shadows.

Leila sat cross-legged on a mat on the kitchen floor happily dipping her rotis into her fish curry with her fingers. She broke a bit of roti, scooped a small amount of coconut sambal on top of it, and popped it into her mouth. It tasted wonderful.

Somehow it tasted so much more delicious than when she had eaten the same meal at lunchtime with Johann, Aunty Sylvie, Mummy and Gran at the big table in the main house. It was much more fun sitting here and eating with Charlotte and Rani and Harold. They were chatting away and laughing about some story Rani was telling, about a young man who wanted to marry her younger sister, without anyone in either family suggesting it, and without even checking their horoscopes. Harold thought he must be mad. Rani thought he was just crazy about her sister. Rani said something else that Leila didn't understand, but might have been something rude or naughty, because Charlotte gave Rani a stern look and both she and Harold burst out laughing. Then they all stopped talking for a while.

There was an oil lamp burning on the floor in front of them. Leila finished her meal and lay her head in Charlotte's lap. Charlotte stroked her hair and she began to fall asleep listening to the sound of them talking once more; she no longer heard the words, just the lilting, musical sound of their voices. She woke to Charlotte stroking her arm gently. "Come, little one, master's car has come. Time I take you for your bath, you must go to bed soon."

"Can't we just stay here a little longer, Charlotte? Please?"

"Raththaran baba, we must go. Come." Charlotte lifted Leila's head from her lap, sat the little girl up, then stood herself and pulled the child to her feet. "Come."

Leila smiled at her. She knew that Charlotte was right and she did not want any more trouble today, but she did not want to go to the main house and see her mother. However, she did want to see Daddy, and Charlotte said he was home. So, she took her ayah's hand and together they walked slowly towards the house. "Charlotte, do you think that if anything bad happened, I could come with you to your village and live with your family?"

Charlotte stopped walking. She stood still and silent. She did not know what to say. The child had clearly sensed that

117

something ominous was happening. She must be truthful. It was the only way. "No, my Leila. That could not be. You do not belong in a village near jungle."

This was very serious. Leila knew it. Charlotte almost never used her name. "That's alright, Charlotte, I just thought I'd ask." She looked at her feet for a moment then lifted her head and tried again. "I could learn to do village work. Rani says I'm very good at pounding spices, and Harold likes it when I help him too. You wouldn't have to dress me or anything. I could just wear a sarong." Her little voice was racing.

Charlotte let go of her hand and hugged her close, then stood a little way from her and looked at her. "Little one, if I could take you to my village, I would do so. But I cannot. You have mother, father, grandmother. They would miss you."

"You know that's not true! Mummy would be glad if I was gone, she would never miss me."

"I do not know, even she might. People are strange." She took the child's hand once more and they walked together in silence to the house.

There was no one in the back room and so they headed for Leila's bedroom to collect her pyjamas and then on to the bathroom to run her bath. Charlotte knelt by the tub as the little girl played in the water. She soaped the child and washed her as she chatted away with tales of endless imaginings; stories of times by the seaside, and playing in the waves. Charlotte felt a sadness she could hardly bear.

Jeff entered the house and found it empty. Leila must still be in the servants' quarters with Charlotte or perhaps having her bath. "Greta?" She did not answer and was not in their bedroom. He heard laughter from their bathroom and found her buried in bubbles in the bath. He looked at her in surprise. "I thought you'd be dressed by now. Isn't this party starting early? I wasn't planning on showering myself until we get back."

118

"It doesn't matter if we're late. Why don't you come in here with me?"

"I'm sorry, darling. I don't think I'm up to it. I've had a hideous day."

She laughed loudly. "You're always up to it! Come on, you'll be far more relaxed if you do."

He looked at her evenly. "Leila's still awake."

"She'll never wander in here uninvited and Charlotte must be with her by now. We can be quiet." She smiled at him and he began to get aroused. He closed the bathroom door and got undressed, then lowered himself into the bath facing her. "Turn around, I'll massage your back."

He did as she asked and sighed with pleasure as she kneaded the tension in the muscles of his upper back and neck. "That's just amazing."

"I know what you like, don't I?" Her hands moved from his back to his penis and she played with him until his erection was hard. "Why don't you turn around and face me?"

She laughed again as she slid onto him. He sank to lie in the bath as she sat on top of him and moved in unison with him. She was the most amazing lover, lithe and luscious. He had never known anyone like her. He never tired of their lovemaking, though it occurred almost daily. His body began to relax. He pushed her lightly off him as he came. She laughed again as she looked down at him. "Feeling better? Stand up and I'll run the shower." She pulled the plug and the bath emptied as the water from the shower cascaded over both of them. She soaped his back and legs.

He left her in the shower and climbed out to dry himself. He leaned forward and kissed her cheek. "Thank you."

"My pleasure." She meant it. He was a wonderful man; kind, gentle, tender. He had never intruded physically nor said a single vulgar word to her. If he asked her for sex, he did so playfully. She reciprocated with gusto. He let her take the lead whenever she wanted. He was the only man she had ever had sex with apart from Albert, and they were as different as any two men could be. She never ceased to wonder at it.

Jeff sat on their bed and towelled his hair. She was right, he felt so much more relaxed, the best he had felt all day. He began to think of the task he still faced in telling her and decided it could wait until the drive to the party or maybe even the drive home. But that might be too risky. Tell even one person and a story could fly. He had told more than one. He would talk to her in the car. He pulled an evening suit and a white dress shirt from the large wooden almirah that ran the length of one wall of their room, chose a bow tie from his chest of drawers and started to dress.

Greta appeared behind him draped in a towel. She let the towel fall, tied his bow tie for him, then opened a jewel box on their dressing table, chose a pair of cufflinks and fastened his shirt cuffs. She stood back and looked at him admiringly. He gazed at the beauty of her naked body and felt himself become aroused again. He caressed her cheek. "You'd better get into that dress of yours or we'll never get out of here." He walked to the door. "Give me a shout if you need help with your necklace." She laughed as he left the room.

Leila was sitting in the back room with Charlotte. She ran to her father as he walked in. "Oh Daddy, you're all dressed up!"

"Come here, poppet." He swung her up into his arms and carried her on one hip. "The mistress will be along soon, Charlotte, why don't you attend to anything you need to do in Leila's room? I'll bring her in shortly." Charlotte nodded in gratitude and left. Leila looked at her father earnestly, as she played with a lock of his hair. Daddy was behaving just as differently as Mummy was today, but in a much nicer way of course, because Daddy was much nicer than Mummy. It was a simple fact. He was the sort of person everyone liked. She had even heard the servants talking about it when she was outside the kitchen door and they didn't know she was listening.

They had said he was a very good master and not at all like Rani's previous master who was very nasty to her in some way, even though he was also Sinhalese.

She had never heard anyone say anything really bad about her mother. But they didn't need to. Without understanding it consciously she registered the difference in their ways of being around her mother; how they spoke to her, being so careful with their words and their voices, even the way they stood and held their bodies seemed to change as soon as her mother came into a room: they were all on guard. It made her feel a little better about how scared she was of her mother, if other people watched how they behaved around her. Come to think of it, Gran was also completely different around Mummy. Only Daddy, Uncle Kingsley, Aunty Sylvie, Johann and some other friends of her parents could be relaxed in her mother's company. It was a strange thing and hard to understand.

Her father carried her to the bookcase near the wall. "Would you like me to read you a story?" He winked at her. There was nothing she enjoyed more. He chose the Brothers Grimm's book of fairy stories, a constant favourite, and sat Leila on his lap to read.

They had looked at the right number of pictures and were just beginning the story when Greta appeared. "I do need that hand, Jeff." She stopped midway in the room, some distance from them and held her necklace out in front of her. She raised one eyebrow in annoyance. "Do we really have time for stories?"

Jeff lifted Leila off his lap and sat her back on the chair. He moved over to Greta, took the necklace from her and fastened it. He kissed her neck and smiled at her as he walked back to Leila. "Of course, we do! We have time for everything today and the party will still be there." He checked his watch and feigned surprise. "If we were to leave right now we'd be most unfashionably on time!"

Greta adjusted her necklace and played with her earrings but she did not challenge him. "Alright, I'll just go check my make-up. Only one story!"

He smiled back at her playfully. "Of course."

She was at the door when she stopped and walked back to them. She leant forward and kissed Leila on the cheek. "Goodnight, Leila, be good and do what Charlotte says."

"I will, Mummy, goodnight." It was their usual farewell if her parents were going out. Maybe her mother had forgotten that she was mad with Charlotte today. Maybe it was just a strange day and everything would be back to normal tomorrow.

CHAPTER SIX

Colombo 1957

Greta de Zylva was nineteen years old when she first noticed Jeff van Buuren as he walked past the pew in which she sat at the back of the Dutch Reformed Church in Bambalapitiya. He was talking with a friend and his deep rich laugh rang out, reverberating in the coolness of the church with its aged stone walls and wooden pews. It was in such contrast with the reverent, muted conversations going on around her as the congregation waited for the service to begin. He sat down two rows in front of her on the opposite side of the aisle where she found she could observe him very well indeed. Then the totally unexpected happened; he began to affect her physically. Whenever she looked at him she felt hot. She put her hands to her face. What if she was blushing?

What was more, everyone around her was oblivious to the fact, and the cause of this violent reaction in her did not seem to know she existed. The Easter service began. She focused on the steady voice of the minister. She suddenly noticed the giant urns overflowing with extravagant tropical blooms that rested on wooden pedestals on either side of the pulpit. The booming voice went on and on, declaring its message of death and rebirth, of suffering and redemption.

She had not felt attracted to any man since her devastating relationship with Albert, if indeed that could be called a relationship. She had tried socialising with school friends for a time after school ended, had attended social events and dances. But the strain of meeting young men and attempting to talk to them had been too much for her. She found that the attention of boys and men of a similar age soon distressed and eventually angered her. She felt on edge with them and annoyed in their company. Her contempt for them then grew, she thought them stupid and treated them rudely, but they pursued her all the more. She began to avoid social situations completely, and had studiously kept away from any male who showed the slightest interest in her since that time.

Her mother had worried constantly about her and told no one about her relationship with Albert. She had even seemingly managed to silence Cynthia. Greta's life at home had improved markedly when Cynthia and Ernest married. Her mother left her largely to her own devices or attempted to help her where she could. Emma had even found her work. Greta had finished school, attended secretarial college and begun her working life typing correspondence and legal letters for Bertram Smith, an elderly lawyer whose wife had been a customer of her mother's.

Both he and his wife now played bridge with her mother, had become her friends. He was heading for retirement and had been very pleased when Greta was able to fill in for his long-term secretary when she went on holiday. He had offered her full-time work not long after, when his secretary retired. He was always polite and kind. His clients were mostly men in his age group and she was surprised and relieved to find that none of them wanted to flirt with her, or even talk to her much at all. They came to see him and seemed content with their experience. She felt safe working for him.

Her life was restricted to the bounds of home, work, an occasional meeting with the few girlfriends who had not abandoned her, and visits to church at Easter and Christmas. Cynthia was currently pregnant and struggling with it. She had become demanding of their mother's attention once more. Her increasingly frequent visits had begun to intrude into the relative isolation and harmony that Greta had found in her way of life with her mother; for Emma spent much of her time working or playing bridge with a circle of friends she had developed, feeling at a loss to know how else to help her younger daughter.

The service was ending. He stood and walked past her with his friend, the two of them deep in conversation. He laughed again, a loud natural laugh. She felt strangely sad, then buoyantly happy. Why did he affect her so? She had sat on her own at the back of the church to avoid unnecessary conversation with people she neither knew nor liked, or both. Her mother, Cynthia and Ernest had gone to sit near the front and would soon come her way, if not someone more difficult like Aunt Inez and Uncle Edward. For a long time she had dreaded meeting Albert at church, but it was clear that he attended another congregation these days, if he attended church at all. He must fear some confrontation with her. The thought pleased her, though the idea of ever being in his presence again both frightened her and filled her with revulsion. Why was she thinking of him? He was to have no place in her life or thoughts. It was the only way she could hold her head high in the world, make herself put one foot in front of the other.

She gathered herself and stood, moving into the throng in the aisle that spilled out of the church and onto the large area of lawn in front of it. Children ran to greet their parents as the wooden doors of the Sunday school building next to the church opened. All around her was a throng of friends and families talking and laughing. Someone took her arm and kissed her cheek, Miriam de Vos. They had not seen each other in months.

"I've called you three times in the last week, Greta. I know you're a recluse these days, but you could have the decency to call me back."

"I got one message, Mimi."

125

"Well, I'll give you that. There was no answer the other two times." Miriam laughed.

Greta heard another laugh and turned her head. "Do you know who that is?"

Miriam followed her gaze. "Which one? The fairer one is Jeff van Buuren, the other is Kingsley Joachim. Beautiful, aren't they? Look all you like, but I'm pretty sure they're out of our league."

"Why do you say that?"

"Well, they're both lawyers and recently back from England. But mostly because they're a good ten years older than us. Plenty of boys our own age to go around, without chasing Colombo's two most eligible bachelors!" Miriam giggled loudly. "I'm not joking! That's what my cousin Heather called them. Hilarious, isn't it? But she's five years older than us and desperate that she's going to miss out." She became distracted. "Look, there's Shirley Milgram with her gorgeous brothers. Why don't we go join them?"

"You go, Mimi, I have to find Mum. Cynthia and Ernest are coming for lunch."

"It's me, Greta. I know just how keen you are to see Cynthia." She gave her friend a meaningful look. "Call me this week. I'm not going to let you hide away!"

* * *

It was two weeks later that Jeff first noticed Greta. He was walking on Galle Face Green watching the children fly their kites on this lovely stretch of grass where land meets sea. He was due to have lunch with Kingsley at the neighbouring Galle Face Hotel in half an hour but had come early to walk. He listened to the lulling sound as the waves gently crashed on the shore. The breeze touched his face and he remembered keenly walking here with his parents as a young child, flying his kite oh so high. He stood and contemplated buying kadalei from one of the many vendors at their mobile carts that served as stalls.

It would spoil his lunch but it was a childhood favourite and the smell was enticing. He was focused on his dilemma when he bumped into someone. They both almost toppled but he found his feet rapidly and caught her arm holding her upright. "I'm so sorry, blundering around and not looking where I'm going!"

Once he was sure she had her footing he took a step back and a long look at the most stunning girl he had ever set eyes on. She was petite yet shapely with a perfect complexion and deep green or were they blue eyes that stared up into his with a mild air of amusement. Greta fought to stop her voice from trembling, to maintain her charade of detachment. "The kadalei smells delicious, doesn't it?"

"My very thought. Let me buy you some?"

"That would be lovely, thank you …"

"Jeff. Jeff van Buuren." He held out his hand.

She smiled as she took it. "Greta de Zylva."

He felt deeply aroused the moment she touched him. It was quite unexpected.

He shook her hand briefly and let it fall. He looked ahead and they walked slowly side by side to the nearest cart. She seemed quite young and yet he was the one who was behaving awkwardly, fascinating. No one had ever affected him this way before. The vendor with his checked sarong and long hair tied up in a kondai smiled and pointed to the different varieties of kadalei available. They each chose their favourite and he expertly wound small paper cones which he filled with the delicious smelling mix of toasted split peas, chilli, and spices. Greta tipped some into her mouth as Jeff paid. She stepped back rapidly, turned her head and spat it out on the ground. She began fanning her mouth.

"How to make a good first impression?" She attempted a smile as she looked up at him. She sensed he would not judge her. Strange that she felt so at ease with him, despite her excitement at their meeting and the awkward circumstance.

127

"Are you alright? Have you burnt your mouth?" He looked at her with concern.

She smiled. "I'll survive."

"I'm meeting a friend for lunch at the Galle Face Hotel, would you care to join us, or at least come and let me buy you a drink to soothe your mouth. I seem to be causing injury upon injury!" He laughed.

She loved the sound of his laugh, that was it. Did it remind her of some other laugh or was it just something to do with him? "What about a drink from that stall instead?" She tipped her head in the direction of another vendor.

He looked genuinely disappointed, but she knew the protocol. He must be curious as to why she was walking alone on the Green, fine for a man, but a Burgher girl must always do so in company or risk a reputation. She would not lie to him. Let him assume she was meeting a friend, or whatever other assumption he might care to make. She knew she could not accept his invitation to lunch, much as she longed to join him. She would not have him think her cheap or easy for the taking. No one would ever think that of her again. She smiled at him. "I'll take a rain check on that lunch, if you're serious?"

He looked at her with a different kind of admiration. She had outmanoeuvred him. He bought her a drink and asked for her phone number. They shook hands briefly in parting.

She had asked Bertram Smith about him, knew where he worked, that he was an up and coming lawyer, that his parents had died suddenly in a car crash and he had returned from the UK to settle their estate and then stayed. She had rung his secretary and pretended to be a potential new client, saying she might have met him at church. His secretary had been most surprised, had volunteered that he didn't usually go to church but rather he and his partner always lunched on Sundays at the Galle Face Hotel. A lucky conversation, and a lucky meeting, as she had not been at all sure how she could enter that prestigious establishment and engineer a meeting with him.

But she had most fortuitously seen him wandering alone and distracted on the Green as she climbed down from her bus. She decided she had best get the next bus home. It would not do to have either he or his friend see her loitering aimlessly.

Jeff entered the foyer of the Galle Face Hotel and wandered through the lovely colonial building, past giant brass urns brimming with red anthuriums flowers, out onto the terrace restaurant. Kingsley had not arrived. He sat at a table with the best view of the ocean. He ordered a drink and sipped it as he watched the light playing on the water and listened to the sound of the seabirds. He felt lighter, more alive than he had felt in months. He realised how weighed down he had been by grief and sadness, no matter the show he made of being happy. How could he be happy with both his parents dead and no chance to say goodbye, with Amy no longer in his life? He stopped himself. He was not going to think about it. He would think instead of the wonderful girl he had just met.

Kingsley studied his friend as he approached the table. Jeff was preoccupied, lost in thought as he gazed out to sea. He looked marvellous. His face was completely relaxed and he looked truly happy, something Kingsley had feared he might never see again. His guilt lessened and he felt a surge of relief, for only six months ago he had done his best to dissuade Amy from considering a life with Jeff in Ceylon, and he had done so in the guise of concern for her welfare. The things he had told her were not untrue: the difficulty in breaking into Burgher society, the complexity of the heightening racial tensions in the island, the unbearable heat prior to the onset of the monsoon. Yet, his emphasis had been styled to deter. She seemed not to realise it. Perhaps the information he fed her paired with her own misgivings gave her pause and added depth to her fear of committing to Jeff. Maybe the intensity of Jeff's grief and distraction in hearing of his parents' death had shocked her. Whatever the reason, she had ended her relationship with Jeff at a time he needed her most. Kingsley's guilt for his part in it had grown as he soon realised he was unable to comfort Jeff in a way she might have.

Kingsley reached the table. "Penny for your thoughts, or maybe a pound? You look very pleased with yourself."

Jeff shifted in his seat as Kingsley sat down opposite him, then looked up, his eyes focused on some distant point. He smiled. "I just met the most ravishing creature." He stopped himself.

Kingsley felt a knot of jealousy and pain surge in his belly, but he was skilled at hiding such emotion. In any case Jeff was not looking at him. He was gazing out to sea. "Tell me?"

"She's simply stunning."

"Anyone I know?"

"I doubt it. She's someone quite new, seems little more than a girl really." He smiled again. "But she is truly splendid." His voice was measured, his tone intense.

Kingsley sensed it at once. Jeff was talking about deep physical attraction to this woman. Here was something quite different. Jeff's attraction to Amy had been far more complex than this; more of the mind and heart. The numerous other women he had dated over the years had all carried the onus of desire. "Do you want me to find out about her?"

Jeff looked at him in surprise. "No, Kingsley. Promise me you'll never do that." He met his friend's eyes. "I'm very serious about this."

Kingsley struggled to hold his gaze, he did not want to reveal himself. They spent most of their time together but rarely ever looked each other in the eye. "You have my word."

* * *

The phone rang and Emma answered it. She walked to Greta's room and knocked on the door. "Greta, there's a call for you. A Jeff van Buuren, he says the two of you have met."

Greta heard the surprise in her mother's voice. No boy had rung her for months and no man had ever telephoned her at home. With Albert, she had done all the calling. How amazing, Jeff could just call her and she could answer. There was no need for guile or shame. All the same she felt intensely anxious as she opened her room door, walked slowly to the hallway table and lifted the receiver. "Hello Jeff."

"Ah, Miss de Zylva! I'm calling to ask you to join me for dinner this Friday, if you would care to?"

"Please don't do that. Don't call me Miss de Zylva. I'm Greta." She didn't want any teasing. She didn't want any games. She was not going to bother with any man who wanted to tease her. Was she overreacting because of the awful way Albert spoke to her, treated her? Jeff had simply called her by the more formal version of her name after all. Was it a sign of respect? Her thoughts were racing and she considered hanging up the phone. It was such a strange reaction, as she was the one who had tracked him down and orchestrated their meeting. She struggled to say anything else.

"Of course, Greta, whatever you prefer. Please forgive my lack of manners, how are you this evening?" His voice was calm and kind.

Her heart stopped racing. She had to find a way to appear normal, not like some schoolgirl and not like someone who knew all the sordid things that she did. She wanted to see him. "I'm very well thank you, Jeff." Her voice was stilted. She persevered. "I'd love to come to dinner with you this Friday."

"Good, good. Do you like to dance?"

"Oh, I love to dance!"

"Splendid. Shall we talk now or leave it for Friday?"

"I think I'd rather get to know you in person." She sighed with relief. She recognised it was a good response. It sounded mature.

They organised a time, she gave him her address and hung up the phone. He was planning to take her out somewhere

where they could dine and dance with others. What a wonderfully normal thing. She felt like crying. She walked quietly into the lounge room and sat down on the sofa. She didn't notice her mother sitting at the small table in the corner of the room, putting the final touches to a garment by hand. They sat in silence for some minutes until Emma could no longer contain her curiosity. "So, Greta, Jeff van Buuren?"

* * *

They were seated at a table beside the dance floor in the Silver Faun Nightclub eating crab curry and watching couples glide skilfully on the silky surface, the imported polished beams, of the sunken wooden dance floor before them. The Louis Moreno Band was in fine form; the tempo of the music swelled and receded; contemporary classics gave way to the complexity of slow jazz. Greta felt her feet ache to dance. She finished her meal and glanced across the table at Jeff as he leaned back in his seat, his focus on the dancers. Her mother had made her a wonderful after-five dress of deep blue satin. She knew she looked lovely, but it was not enough surely, for a man like this. She had let him steer the conversation on the drive here. What could she say to rouse his interest, show him she was not some inept child?

He turned towards her and caught her eye. He smiled slowly. "Shall we?" He rose and held out his hand. It was all so seamless, something he must have done countless times before with other women.

"With pleasure." She realised she needed to settle down or leave. She hoped her hand would not tremble. She must not spoil this opportunity. His hand was on her back guiding her gently onto the dance floor, then taking one hand firmly while his other arm encircled her waist. The miraculous happened, she relaxed. She found that her body followed his lead perfectly. This was as it was meant to be and so unlike the measured plodding of the young men at the series of debutante parties she had forced herself to attend when school ended. She realised that she felt safe with him. She began to enjoy herself.

The roof of his Riley was folded down and the moist warm air wafted over her as they cruised along the still crowded streets. People walked in couples or small groups along the sides of the road as fireflies danced around them. She glanced down a side street and saw a group of young boys playing cricket. It was nearly midnight. They had danced for hours. She did not want to reach her home, did not want this night to end. She feared it was all she may ever have. She had no right to such happiness. Her relationship with Albert must surely mean this could not be.

He pulled up in front of her house and turned the engine off. He looked at her and stroked her cheek. "Thank you, Greta. It's been a long time since I've enjoyed myself so much."

She lifted her chin and looked him directly in the eye. "Thank you, Jeff. It's been the most wonderful evening I've ever had."

A wave of complex emotion passed across his face. She could not fathom it. There was both sadness and happiness in it. "Come, I'll walk you to your door." He opened her car door for her, then guided her along the path to her porch, as he had guided her all night on the dance floor. She loved the feel of his hand on her back or at her waist. She turned in his arms at her front door and he leaned forward and kissed her gently on her mouth. "I'll call you tomorrow." That was it. He was walking away. He had not tried to touch her anywhere else. She brushed her hand against her lips as she watched him climb into his car, then turned her key and pushed the front door open.

* * *

"We're planning on calling the baby Jacob, after Ernest's father, if it's a boy, or Emily in honour of you, if it's a girl." Cynthia looked at her mother intently, determined to capture

133

her attention. A hard thing to do as Emma kept moving around the room, arranging cushions, straightening the table cloth, adjusting the serviettes in their rings. "Mum! Are you listening?"

"What? Oh, that's lovely Cynthia, really lovely. The name will still be quite hers then, won't it?" Emma was on tenterhooks. Jeff van Buuren had asked her for Greta's hand in marriage after knowing her for only six weeks. Greta had accepted him. There was nothing she could do about it, nor did she wish to. She could not imagine a finer match for Greta. He was a kind man and an honourable one. If anyone could make Greta feel safe or loved he would be able to.

She was dreading this family lunch. It ought to be a time of celebration and happiness; one daughter about to give birth to her first grandchild, the other announcing her engagement. But her daughters were not, and would never be, close. She recognised that some of it was her doing. She had made too much of a difference between them in childhood, had loved them very differently and tried later to compensate. Strange that Cynthia, the one she had loved most always, was now so insecure and competitive with her younger sister. Yet, there it was. How life would have turned out if Jürgen had lived she had no idea. He had plummeted to his death on a treacherous road in the hill country after drinking late into the night only two years after she left him. At that time, she had felt both sadness and relief; he could never again make any claim on her daughters.

She had found herself thinking very differently in the last few years, ever since Greta's horrible liaison with Albert van den Berg. She was convinced that even a drunken and dissolute Jürgen would have been a deterrent to Albert. Perhaps, all the more so, because of his unpredictable behaviour. She did not at any time wish him back in her life. Yet she longed to have someone with whom to share the burden of parenthood. The likelihood that the estrangement between her daughters was mostly of her making was hard to bear.

Greta had sworn her to secrecy, wanted to make the announcement herself. This felt so unwise, as she might have prepared Cynthia for a difficult reality. Jeff was wealthier than Ernest, older, more educated, a far better catch. She hoped that Cynthia would cope. She and Ernest had been told of Greta's relationship with Jeff only two weeks ago. They were here to meet him for the first time. She decided to temper the waters before Greta joined them. "Ernest, have you ever met Jeff? In some work context perhaps? Or at church?"

"No, Mrs de Zylva. I'm afraid not. I think we move in different circles." Ernest looked at her with his candid open face. He had no guile. "I've asked around. He's well respected. That's all I know. I'll be pleased to tell you what I think of him later this afternoon." He felt some responsibility for Greta's welfare, as the only man in the family. Cynthia had never told him that Greta had had an abortion, or about Albert. She had been too ashamed and frightened that he might not marry her if he knew at the time, and later that he would be wounded by her lack of trust in not having told him.

"That's fine, Ernest. I was just asking out of curiosity. I like Jeff very much, in the little time I've spent with him."

"Stop fretting, Mum, it's pretty unlikely we'll get to know him well at all. A man like that isn't going to be with Greta for long!"

"Cynthia! That's so unkind." Emma felt dismayed. This was going to be even more difficult than she had anticipated.

Ernest looked at his wife with surprise and distaste. But he quickly excused her. She was in her last month of pregnancy after all. He had heard that women must be forgiven almost anything at such a time.

Greta stood in the doorway looking at her sister with contempt. She felt an inner glow of triumph. She savoured the moment. Let Cynthia be as foul as she could be, no matter. Jeff would be here soon enough and they would make their announcement together. Then they would see what happened.

135

She was determined she would not be the one to lose her composure. She must not let herself be baited by Cynthia, in any way. No matter what her sister might say she must keep her head, behave well. She felt sure that Cynthia would not mention Albert. It would be too risky. But even that must somehow be treated coolly, if it did come out. She steeled herself.

The doorbell rang. Greta turned and walked with measured steps along the narrow hallway. She reached the front door and opened it. He smiled at her. He bent and kissed her lightly on the lips, then let their kiss linger. She pulled away gently. "Jeff, I think you should know that my sister Cynthia and I are not close. This may be difficult."

He smiled again. There was so much warmth and reassurance in that smile. "You said she's expecting and almost due? We'll take no notice of anything untoward then, shall we?"

Yes, ignore Cynthia if she decided to be spiteful. How disempowering for her. It matched well with her own resolve. She felt less on guard. She took his hand. He was truly on her side, her ally, something she had not had in her family since her childhood, since they had left Anesha and her father behind.

Emma was still on her feet and moved to greet Jeff as they entered the room. "Come in, Jeff. Please come in and meet my older daughter Cynthia and her husband Ernest Jansz."

Jeff kissed Emma in greeting. "I'm so glad to be here, Mrs de Zylva." He turned to Cynthia who remained seated. He bent to kiss her on the cheek. "Cynthia, my pleasure." He shook Ernest's hand without contest. "Ernest." He was warm. He was confident. A stranger might assume he was the host welcoming visitors, putting them at their ease.

Greta had been standing back. She moved to his side and took his hand. She led him to an armchair that faced the couch on which Cynthia and Ernest were seated. She and Emma sat on upright chairs that had been arranged alongside the armchair. They sat in a semi-circle and the warmth of his greeting gave way to silence. The moments passed. Jeff sat calmly, waiting to see what would develop. Greta, beside him, felt his calmness, and remained silent.

Cynthia was deeply aware of a sense of irritation. This man was too handsome, too at ease, too confident. It made her feel awkward. Ernest looked like an overgrown schoolboy beside him. Greta was a different being in his company; settled, content, beautiful. Cynthia's annoyance grew. She felt clumsy, bloated, cumbersome. How unfortunate to meet someone like him, from a different tier of society, in her present condition. She comforted herself with the conviction that he was a temporary acquaintance. Someone who would soon move on. She need not invest her scant energy at this difficult time in being any more than superficially polite. She would get through this lunch. Fine beads of perspiration were breaking out on her nose and cheeks. The air from the circling fan above them was not enough to cool her. She unfurled a paper fan by her side and fanned herself vigorously. Ernest looked at her with concern. He reached for the fan, but she snapped it closed and batted his hand away in irritation, barely knowing what she was doing. He pulled his hands to his sides looking hurt and abashed.

Emma felt the pressure of being hostess. It coupled with her anxiety about the impending announcement. She searched for a neutral topic to ease the company into pleasant conversation, but this eluded her. She steadied herself. She had, after all, needed to negotiate challenging social situations most of her life. She must do it again now for both of her daughters' sakes. Far better Greta and Jeff just make their announcement and get it done with. "So, Jeff, I hope you like lamprais? They're in the oven warming up now. I ordered them especially for the occasion."

"Excellent choice, Mrs de Zylva. They smell wonderful. One of my favourites." He took her cue and turned to Greta.

She nodded. "Cynthia, Ernest." She paused, looking directly at her sister first but turning her gaze to look at Ernest as she continued. "Jeff and I would like you to share our good news ... We're engaged."

Ernest rose immediately and in a few steps bent to kiss Greta. "Congratulations!" He shook Jeff's hand vigorously. "Wonderful news, wonderful. Welcome to the family." He stood back and smiled at them both, then turned to his wife who was still silent. Cynthia looked so pale, he felt worried about her. Might she faint? She had never done so before, but he had been warned that this could happen in pregnancy. Maybe this excitement was too much for her.

Cynthia was struggling. This was simply insufferable. Greta to marry a man with wealth and social standing that she could never attain? Greta who was damaged goods, soiled, spoiled. It felt unbearable. She longed to tell this foolish man that he had been taken in by her sister. Yet, how could she without tarnishing her own reputation and risking her marriage? She struggled with her desire to scream it out. They were all looking at her. She had to say something. She tried but could not utter the needed words of felicitation. In the end she could bear it no longer. "And when is baby due?"

"Cynthia!" Emma looked at her daughter with both shock and concern.

Ernest was staring at her in amazement, dumbfounded that she could ask such an insulting and taboo question of any engaged couple, least of all her younger sister and her fiancé.

Jeff looked at Cynthia with deep distaste. So, this was the calibre of his future sister-in-law. Greta had not been wrong. He turned to her and patted her hand lightly. "Darling, it's a little stuffy in here, don't you think? Shall we step outside for a walk, a breath of fresh air?" He turned to Emma. "Will you excuse us, Mrs de Zylva? We won't be long, I'm looking forward to those lamprais."

"Of course, Jeff, of course. I'll turn the oven off and they'll stay warm. Take your time."

He stood and held his arm to Greta. She took it and they left without a word to Cynthia. They heard hurried footsteps following. Ernest caught them at the front door. "I'm so very sorry. I don't know what's the matter with Cynthia today. Please forgive her, I'm sure it's just her condition."

Jeff looked at him steadily. "We won't be long, Ernest. Please ask your wife to keep a civil tongue, if she can. This is an important day for us."

They walked slowly down the street hand in hand and into the next street. Jeff stopped walking. "She's jealous of you, darling. You know that, don't you?" Greta remained silent. He put his hand under her chin and lifted her head to look into her eyes. "How awful to have a sister like that. Makes me glad to be an only child when I see this sort of thing."

He was making it sound so ordinary, as if this happened in other families too, as if it was all Cynthia's fault. But they were standing only a few metres away from a large flowering tree with overhanging branches. It reminded her of the tree that Albert had pulled her under, where he had started fondling her breasts, at the time when she was getting to know him, when she was still excited by him, before things became so terrible. What if Cynthia ever said more? She wanted to leave with Jeff now, to forget about lunch with her family. But she knew that Cynthia would see this as a sign of weakness. She had to return to her home and face her sister.

They were all seated at the table. Cynthia had said no word of apology. She had, in fact, said no word at all since Greta and Jeff returned. She sat fanning herself on the couch and insisted Ernest make a fuss of her and help move her to the table when Greta and Jeff seated themselves there at Emma's urging. Emma and Elly rushed to and fro, bringing warmed plates from the kitchen to place in front of each of them. Finally, Emma sat at the head of the table and Elly entered with a large platter piled high with lamprais. She placed it ceremoniously in the centre of the table and left.

139

The aroma of the food was rich and enticing. Emma gestured to the platter and they each helped themselves to one of the small rectangular parcels of food wrapped and baked in a banana leaf. The bamboo pin that held the leaf in place was removed and each leaf unfurled to reveal its contents: glistening ghee rice adorned with meat and vegetable curries, crumbed meat balls and a selection of sambals , the flavours of each enhancing the others, melding wonderfully after being baked together. They began to eat in silence, clearly savouring the food, if not some of the company.

Jeff thought of his own mother who ordered lamprais for any special occasion. He turned to Emma. "Delicious, Mrs de Zylva, truly delicious. Thank you. It's a real celebration."

Emma smiled with relief. "I'm so glad you're enjoying them, Jeff, please help yourself to more."

Ernest saw his chance. He raised his wine glass. "Once more, congratulations to you both."

He and Emma drank a toast while Cynthia sipped reluctantly at her glass of water in a show of civility, eyes down and avoiding anyone's gaze. In truth no one looked her way. She had been convinced that Jeff and Greta would not return for the meal and was most surprised and somewhat chastened by the fact that they had.

She realised that she had to do something. A direct apology was more than she could bear. Her barbed question was obviously well off-target. Jeff's reaction made it clear that he thought her crass and vicious. So, Greta must be behaving very differently with him than she had with Albert, playing the innocent no doubt. It did not occur to her that Jeff might be treating Greta with a level of care and respect that Albert van den Berg was incapable of. In her eyes her sister was entirely to blame for what had happened to her in her relationship with Albert, no matter the difference in their age, power or status. She had spent her life blaming Greta and her father for the unhappiness in her family. She had no other lens with which to view her sister.

Cynthia lifted her head and looked briefly at both Greta and Jeff with as casual an air as she could muster. She worked hard to keep her tone of voice light. "So, have you set a date as yet?"

Greta was taken by surprise. Jeff answered. "No, no we haven't." He squeezed Greta's hand under the table. "But it might be a fine time to decide." He glanced in Greta's direction. "What do you say to two months from now? That should give us enough time to organise things?" He had no idea what organising a wedding might entail. But after meeting her sister he longed to get Greta out of her family environment, to have her safely in his house where he could make sure she had a good life. Besides that, he was tired of waiting. She was clearly not interested in anything more than a kiss before marriage, and lovely though kisses were, he wanted her, the sooner the better.

Greta felt ambushed. She had not the slightest doubt when she said yes to Jeff's proposal of marriage. She may have known him a few short weeks, but she trusted him, was at ease with him in a way she had not thought possible. Yet to marry in two months? She felt all their eyes on her. She would much rather marry in six months' time. But to say this now, in front of her family? He clearly thought he was coming to her rescue in suggesting this early marriage. Her eyes had been down, contemplating the table as he spoke, giving nothing away. She lifted her head. "Yes, I think two months from now would be a fine time."

Cynthia had sensed Greta's hesitation. She turned to her mother. "So, Mum, you'll be making the bride's dress and going away outfit?" She glanced up at Greta, including her. Greta felt angry. She was not going to be pushed into anything more by Cynthia's bullying. It had gone on all her childhood.

141

She was going to have a different life with Jeff and it needed to start now. "I'll sort that out with Mum soon enough, Cynthia. We are going to be very busy organising everything in such a short time." She looked at her sister's pregnant belly pointedly. "I'm sure you'll have your hands full too and will understand why I can't ask you to be matron of honour?"

* * *

"I can't stand still another second. I'm sweltering. Just get this thing off me!" Greta was on the verge of shouting. She felt like a trapped animal. She stared at the image in the mirror before her. The dress was exquisite; the ivory satin hugged her body and cascaded from her waist, the lace at the neckline hid her cleavage, accentuated the colour of her skin. She realised that she looked lovely in it, but waves of nausea hit her as she studied her reflection. She averted her eyes. What was she doing? How would she get through this? Virginal white, a tradition that had to be adhered to. No one knew, apart from her mother and Cynthia and Albert, and of course that butcher, who called himself a doctor, somewhere in Colombo. But he had never known her name. Could she carry this off? Would she get away with it?

Emma, kneeling beside her daughter, focused on the gown and continued to pin. She hoped this was the final fitting. Greta appeared more distressed each time, the closer the dress came to completion. "Hold still, Greta, I'm nearly done. With any luck this will be it, and the next time you try it on it will be done." She spoke calmly. She felt her daughter's terror and understood it. So sad that it came at the prospect of marrying a kind and caring man. She was suddenly, unexpectedly flooded by the memory of having her own bridal dress fitted. Martha Ferdinands had made the dress for her. She had been so excited about each fitting, had felt no apprehension about marrying Jürgen, just a desire to escape Colombo and her life there.

Emma fervently wished a good life for Greta, a far better life than the one she had thrown herself into. This decision to marry was just as rapid as her own had been. Yet, Cynthia and Ernest had married hastily and were managing well. Little Jacob had been born, and Ernest's mother had employed a good ayah. It meant she could enjoy her visits with her first grandchild and not worry about Cynthia and whether she was coping or not. She found herself devoting her time between visiting one daughter and her new baby, and organising a wedding for the other. Jeff was paying for almost everything to do with the wedding. Her daughters were fortunate, and so was she. Others could give them what she could not.

It should be a good time of life. Yet, Greta was unravelling before her. She seemed to have lost the slow-won confidence that working for Bertram Smith had brought her. She was still going to work and planned to continue once she returned from her honeymoon. Both Bertram and Emma thought it unlikely. Bertram was quietly searching for a new secretary. Greta had not spoken with Jeff of her intention to keep working. She had, in reality, discussed very little with Jeff apart from some details of the wedding, the guest list and the fact she would be living in his home once they were married. He was keeping their honeymoon destination a surprise.

Greta didn't really care about the wedding, except that it be a small affair. The details didn't matter. Let Jeff and her mother organise it. A church wedding, a luncheon reception at the Galle Face Hotel, let him choose. They'd invite his friends. He seemed to have no family. They'd invite some necessary relations from her side, some of her mothers' friends, a few girl-friends from school. Miriam de Vos was to be her bridesmaid, Kingsley Joaquim Jeff's best man. None of it really mattered. She'd get through the ceremony and the reception somehow. That part would be all right.

But what would happen after? Surely Jeff would know. What would he think of her? Would he despise her as much as she despised herself, whenever she allowed herself a trace of a memory of her time with Albert? She could call it off, delay it. But she knew if she did that she would lose her nerve and not marry him, may never marry anyone. She had to see it through, somehow. She was agitated. She felt trapped. Yet, to continue her life as a single woman living with her mother felt worse. To attempt to return to a life with those of her own age was impossible. There really was only one course of action.

Emma ended her task with satisfaction. She patted Greta lightly on the leg as she finished pinning. "There, it's done."

"Good! Now get it off me!" Greta began to pull the gown off. She screamed suddenly as a pin pierced her skin. She spun round and looked at her mother with anger and accusation.

Emma felt deeply hurt, but she knew she must not let herself be silenced. She could so easily fall into a place from which it was very hard to return; where any communication felt too much of an effort. It was a way of responding to hurtful behaviour that had ended in disaster in her relationship with Greta's father. "Here. Just slip your arm out. Good." Emma helped her daughter undress. She kept her tone as steady as she could. "Greta, I don't think I can keep this up unless you make more of an effort. I'm doing everything I can so that your wedding will be a success. But this rudeness has to stop!"

Greta looked at her mother in the mirror, as she helped ease the dress off her shoulders. She noticed that her mother's hair was streaked with silvery strands and just how tired and worn-out she looked. She looked old. Not as old as Bertram Smith or his wife, but too old for someone still in her forties. Odd, she had never seen this before. She felt a sudden unexpected surge of fear at the thought that her mother might die. But it passed in a moment, replaced by her familiar comforting rage. Good, her mother deserved to look old before her time. If not for her mother, her father might be here to give her away. Instead she must walk down the aisle on the arm of a stand-in, Bertram Smith, her employer, a good man, but a very poor second.

Her mother folded the gown over her arm as Greta stood, still facing the mirror. She looked at Emma in reflection. "I'll give it my best try." The edge of mockery in her voice hung between them. Emma turned silently away.

* * *

It was the morning of the wedding. Miriam de Vos was due to arrive at any moment. The bridal cars would be there in half an hour. Greta had refused to come out of her bedroom. She had not eaten breakfast. Emma stood outside her door and knocked gently once more. Elly peered at Emma from the kitchen door and shook her head slowly. Emma knew that Elly was finding it as hard as she was to tolerate Greta's pre-wedding nerves and rude behaviour, even though most of this had been turned her way, since Greta and Elly rarely spoke to each other directly at all. They did not like each other; equally there was no true animosity between them, more a sense of disapproval on Elly's side and indifference for Greta's part. Emma was eternally grateful that Elly had been away on the day of Greta's abortion. She appeared to know nothing about it. A most fortunate thing, as it also meant that no other servants in Colombo or their employers would know.

Elly turned and headed back to the kitchen. She began to clear away the breakfast she had made for the young mistress. It had been cold for hours and there would be no time for her to eat it now. The young mistress had always been difficult, and she felt the mistress had been much too lenient with her, especially when she was younger and out visiting her girlfriends all the time. She had been far more docile in recent years, since Miss Cynthia married and moved away. But in the last few weeks her behaviour to the mistress had been intolerable.

No one in her own family would ever dare to speak so rudely to a parent. She had often got a sharp slap on the face from her mother if she dallied at all, and she dared not think what would have happened had she contradicted her. While she did not approve of her treatment by her own family and had very much appreciated Emma's kindness to her, she was none the less sure that her mistress was far too soft with Greta. Now it was too late. The young mistress had been spoiled. She thought too highly of herself. She would never bend to her husband's will. She did not hold out much hope for the success of this marriage.

Emma knocked firmly at the closed door this time. "Greta, you have to come out. Miriam will be here." There was no answer.

Slowly the door swung open and Greta stood staring at her mother, dressed in her wedding dress with a terrified expression on her face. "I can't do this. We'll have to call it off." Her bluster was gone, her voice was soft.

"Really, Greta? You really want to give up this chance for happiness?"

Greta reached for her mother's arm and dragged her into her bedroom, closing the door behind them. Emma was too stunned to resist. Greta rarely touched her. "You know why Mum, you know ..." She began to sob, highpitched gasping sobs.

Emma took her daughter's hand gently. She sat on the bed and Greta sank down beside her. "What if he finds out, Mum?" Greta's sobbing lessened, her voice steadied. "You don't know what Albert did to me ..."

Emma placed her arm tentatively around her daughter's shoulders. Greta did not shrug it off. "I am sure that you will not be the only one who has experience in the matter, Greta." Emma had no doubt. Jeff was too popular, too confident for it to be otherwise. "Jeff is a kind man. Let him be kind to you." They sat in silence. Emma's face clouded. Had she ever known tenderness? Passion yes, so much passion, at the start with Jürgen. But tenderness? No, she didn't think so. Yet, this was what she wished for her troubled daughter, more than anything. It might offer hope.

* * *

The collar of her chiffon going-away dress fluttered against her neck as the car sped along the narrow road, then slowed again. A bullock cart pulled over to the left, ever so slightly, and Jeff eased the car skilfully past, so as not to startle the ambling animal or its load. The driver saluted them with a wave of gratitude as they passed. They drove through another village with its thatched huts. A row of men squatted by the roadside chewing betel nut and spitting the residue on the ground beside them, their mouths stained the same bright red as their spittle. The car rounded the corner and the ocean came into view once more, this time glanced through a grove of coconut palms.

Greta felt her body begin to relax. She had rarely travelled out of Colombo; a few holidays with girlfriends, an occasional trip to Negombo with her mother to visit a great aunt. It was wonderful to leave the city behind. She had survived the wedding ceremony and the reception. She had little memory of either, just snippets imbued with intense feeling; Bertram Smith steadying her as she clung to his arm on the walk up the aisle, Jeff guiding her around to talk with people at the reception. Inez and Edward had been over friendly in a strange proprietary way, as though her successful marriage to Jeff was somehow their doing, as though she were in some way theirs. Cynthia had been civil, hiding behind her preoccupation with Jacob, while Ernest seemed genuinely happy for her. Miriam was simply in awe of Jeff, and even more so of Kingsley, as she sat beside him at the reception and attempted conversation. Yes, Kingsley, she remembered Kingsley, he was definitely memorable. He had congratulated her warmly, genuinely. He had treated Miriam well, attempted to put her at ease. He seemed truly happy for Jeff, though in some strange intense way sad as well. Could it be possible that he had feelings for her?

They reached the coastal town of Bentota and pulled into a beachside rest house. Jeff felt his excitement and desire grow. The wedding had been a success; the low-key affair that they both clearly wanted. Greta had been so nervous all day. No, she had been that way since they announced their engagement. The last few weeks had sped by with no flicker of doubt to colour his certainty. Emma had organised the wedding and reception. He had planned the honeymoon; a slow two-week sojourn along the southern coast of the island from Bentota beach to the walled Portuguese city of Galle, on to Tissa by the lake and finally to Yala National Park. She would love it. He was sure. So much to show her of the island he loved, and that she had barely seen.

He turned to her. He stroked her cheek. "Here we are, darling, the beginning of our trip." He laughed. "Our life together!" She looked at him intensely but said nothing. Their courtship had been so brief, she was so lovely. He leant forward and kissed her, a deeper kiss than ever before. The porter opened Greta's door for her. She climbed out and stood by the car. She watched as he called two young men dressed in sarongs and short-sleeved checked shirts who took their bags from the boot and carried them in. She wondered at it, surely one of them could have managed both suitcases easily? Jeff handed the porter the keys. He left the car to be parked and put his arm around her as they made their way to reception. He led her from there to the lovely first-floor suite that was theirs for this first night of their honeymoon; spacious and panelled in mahogany with windows that opened to look out to sea and gauze curtains that billowed with the evening breeze.

"Are you hungry? Do you want to have an early dinner?"

"No, not now." She was standing by the windows gazing at the sea and the air played with folds of dappled colour in the skirt of her dress: sea green, pale blue, purple, pink. What an unusual, gorgeous fabric. The golden light of evening made her skin glow and her thick brown hair shimmer auburn as she turned to him. He reached for her and pulled her gently into his arms. He unzipped her dress as he held her close, then lifted it lightly over her head. She pulled away from him and he watched as she sat on the edge of the bed in her ivory silk slip, slowly rolling her stockings down her lovely legs.

He felt a surge of happiness that matched his growing desire. He unbuttoned his shirt and tossed it onto the floor at the foot of the bed. He sat to remove his shoes. She had climbed up on the bed behind him and was hugging him around the chest, burying her head against the firmness of the muscles of his back. He felt her body tremble. Gently he unclasped the hands that gripped him. He turned and slid her up the bed lying lightly beside her. He caressed her breasts softly, tenderly, through the silken garments she was wearing. His hand moved lightly between her legs and up over her belly. "It's okay, darling, we can stop any time you like. Just tell me."

She stopped trembling and he felt her body relax. She began to writhe with pleasure as his hands moved on, over the contours of her body, seeking to find and know her, revelling in her silkiness. He pulled away from her slightly and stroked her hair with the softest caress. He undressed her slowly, piece by piece, then stood to let his trousers fall. He gazed at the beauty of her naked body; so perfect, so luscious. He was surprised to see her staring back at him, taking in his erection, not so much with curiosity but rather with desire. It excited him all the more.

She had never known such tenderness. His hands and his lips sought her out but never intruded. Her body responded in a way that was new to her. He was not telling her to do anything. She was a partner in this embrace, this dance of ever increasing pleasure and intensity, not watching herself from afar, frozen and obedient, as she had been with Albert. This was something entirely different.

149

They had fallen asleep in each other's arms after their love-making. That was what it had been. Not simply sex. Not something degrading or brutal. Greta woke to this realisation and to a room suffused with golden light. She wondered for a moment where she was. Then she remembered. Jeff was deeply asleep on the bed beside her. The light of the setting sun played through the billowing curtains and threw dancing shadows around the room. She turned to look at him, careful not to wake him. She glanced tentatively at him and looked away. His arm across her body held her tight, his touch imparted surety. She turned to look at him once more and took him in: the dark tousled head, the lean body; she filled herself up with the sight and smell of him. He was her husband. How strange, she barely knew him. Until now she had let her thoughts go no further than this day, unsure if or how she might survive it, terrified that he might realise she was tarnished, reject her. The opposite had happened. He was so gentle, so tender. Yes, she could see herself making a life with him.

CHAPTER SEVEN

Colombo, Friday 25th September 1964

The night air was thick with moisture and warmth as they drove on through streets still alive with people walking and talking, journeying together along the roadside. Jeff had the roof of their Riley rolled down and the wind played with her hair. Greta did not mind. She felt enlivened by the night, by the life around her and by being alone with him at last. Suddenly her mood began to change. She had been excited about the party all day, but a sense of unease and apprehension began to build the closer they came to their destination. Large social gatherings could still intimidate her. They were usually filled with people who Jeff had known for much of his life. She might be accepted and treated well as his wife, but it did not feel sufficient. She longed to be noticed in her own right and her confidence that this would happen suddenly began to wane.

Sheila Leembruggen had been a few years below her at school and she realised that she felt a far greater kinship with her, than with her parents who were Jeff's friends, and the reason for their inclusion on the guest list. She tried to steady herself; there would be dancing, and Kingsley. She would not be left to her own devices, for if Jeff was ever preoccupied by others at such an event, Kingsley would be by her side. She took it for granted and had not thought to ask Jeff whether Kingsley was coming.

The excitement of any party for her revolved around these two possibilities: being seen to be beautiful and dancing all night with her husband or his best friend. In addition, Sylvia Kelly and her husband Frank would be there, and so too Reggie Kumar, another of Jeff's boyhood friends with his wife Rita. All were people she could talk to. The prospect of conversing with others that she knew less well or not at all held no appeal for her beyond simple civility. Her interest in gossip was limited to anything that might impact her personally, she was no good at small talk and felt out of her depth with politics. There seemed little left to be said.

She tried to conjure the image of her entrance in her stunning new dress; it had quietened her nerves all day, transformed them to anticipation. But it failed her now. "Jeff, can we pull over? I just want to sit for a moment before we get there." She had never told him how much her heart could race at times like this.

"Of course." He pulled the car over to the side of the road. He recognised that she was anxious, that she often struggled at large social gatherings, no matter how much she tried to convince herself otherwise. He would never let her know that he saw this. She was too proud. It would wound her.

Perhaps this was his opportunity to broach the critical issue that had preoccupied him all day, though he baulked inwardly at the thought of beginning the conversation. He steeled himself. "Greta, there's something I need to talk to you about." He stopped, and she looked at him with curiosity. He reached for her hand and held it. "It's something I've been trying to find a way to discuss, been thinking about for quite some time now."

"Is it about whether we stay or leave?" She looked at him keenly.

"Yes." So, after all his foreboding they had arrived at the same place after all.

"I've been thinking about it too, though I try not to. I was afraid that that's what this party is about tonight, another farewell announcement! But Sylvia is sure it's an engagement party." She stopped talking. They sat in silence for a few moments.

"To be honest I've done a lot more than think about it. I wrote to a friend of mine, Ronald de Souza, in Australia. I've talked to you about him. He's as good a friend as Kingsley." He watched her as he spoke, but could find no indication of how she was reacting. Her face was calm, impassive. She said nothing. He went on. "He's offered me a place in his law firm in Melbourne. The letter came today."

She sighed deeply and her face clouded. "Oh Jeff, do we really have to leave?"

He squeezed her hand. "I'm afraid we do. And it's not going to be easy. We will have to leave almost all our money behind."

She seemed distracted. He wasn't sure if she had heard his last comment at all. "Yes, Mum thinks it will be dangerous to stay. She thinks there might even be a civil war. She was asking me about our plans this afternoon." She paused. "I told her to go to England and help Cynthia. After all, she has the three boys and Ernest is away with work some of the time." She paused, lost in thought. "I'm pretty sure they got some of their money out." She had heard. "It must be hard though, without servants."

He felt his gratitude to his mother-in-law anew and remembered his own conversation with her. "The situation with taking funds out of the country has worsened a lot since Cynthia and Ernest left. But I don't know why you're worrying about them. Sounds to me like they're doing fine, and I can't imagine Cynthia ever showing a moment's concern for you!" His dislike for her sister was real and evident.

It pleased Greta. "Yes, you're right. Perhaps it might be best if Mum came with us. She could bring in some money with her dressmaking, and she'd be a great help with Leila. She has a lot more patience with her than I do!"

He felt shocked anew by the lack of any affection in her voice, and by the actual distaste that was present as she spoke of the daughter he loved. But he had no idea how to approach the subject, and in any case, this was not the time to challenge her. He remained silent.

She looked at him. "When, Jeff? When do you think we should go?"

"The sooner the better. It will take six months at least, to get our genealogies done, go through our interviews and our health examinations at the Australian High Commission."

"Our genealogies? Why?"

"The 'White Australia Policy', darling. We have to be eighty per cent European, I believe, to qualify."

Her nose wrinkled with distaste. "Why don't we go to England or America instead? They don't have any policy like that, do they? I hate the thought of living somewhere with that kind of prejudice."

"I don't want to go back to England, or Scotland." His face grew solemn.

He had told her that there had been one significant love in his life before he met her. A girl he had known in Scotland. He had never mentioned her name. She was glad he didn't want to return there. In addition, she had no desire to live in the same country or in any real proximity to Cynthia ever again in her life. It made sense not to go to the UK. He continued. "As for the States, my qualifications won't be accepted there, I'd have to sit exams, start from the beginning again."

"Australia ..." She let the word linger. Until now she had said it with anger. Seemingly endless numbers of Burghers had left for its shores. Now she was to be one of them. "How have so many people gone there, if they have this dreadful policy?"

He was amazed by her ignorance. But she avoided anything political. He needed to convince her. "I'm not really sure.

Many of us have British qualifications which are recognised there. And the weather is far warmer than in Britain, even tropical in some regions, although Melbourne is quite temperate I believe with seasons …" His voice trailed off. He was trying to find something that might appeal to her, yet did not want to raise unrealistic expectations.

She seemed distracted. He hesitated: best perhaps to address her chief concern. "Have you considered that we Burghers are quite a prejudiced bunch? Or for that matter just how prejudiced everyone in this island is against anyone who is different to them? The Sinhalese and Tamils don't just differ on religious grounds, they have their own caste systems and endless hierarchies. Everyone seems sure that someone else is in the wrong or is inferior to their own group."

"That's just too grim, Jeff." She had no wider knowledge of island society or of Buddhist or Hindu culture beyond the ordinary spectacle of the major religious events and holidays. She had remained within the tight-knit confines of Burgher society all her life. She had never formed friendships with the Sinhalese or Tamil girls who had attended the same school as her, and who were in any case all Christian, as were the few of Jeff's school friends and colleagues who were either Sinhalese or Tamil.

Both she and Jeff had been raised by Sinhalese ayahs and had lived with Sinhalese servants all their lives, but somehow, she seemed unable to consciously acknowledge this intimate intertwining of cultures at the heart of their family life. Greta had remembered Anesha well when she was a young girl and had even wondered what might have happened to her after her father died. But she never thought to seek her out as an adult. The day to day business of life preoccupied her. Like most Burghers of her time, her own Sinhalese or Tamil ancestry had been largely disavowed rather than embraced; a lie of omission with profound ramifications in terms of both personal and national identity.

155

She tried her best to consider what he was saying, what everyone had been thinking and talking of for months or even years. She had been working hard to ignore it, but somehow it had become the inevitable during the course of this one day. It was clear that both Jeff and her mother were convinced they ought to leave. She began to reconcile herself to the fact and then suddenly embraced it. It became a reality in her mind. She thought of a life without servants, with limited money. They would need all the help they could get.

"Yes, we'd better take Mum. I'll ask her tomorrow. I'm pretty sure she'll come." But she spoke as though it made no difference to her if her mother came or not, that it was merely the expedient thing to do. She had no idea how deeply she still relied on her mother, not just her husband.

"Well, for people who haven't been able to have the conversation, we've got off to a great start! Come on, the Leembruggens know how to throw a party whatever the occasion. Let's enjoy ourselves while we still can." He turned the ignition key and pulled back onto the road.

Their car rolled slowly through the ornate metal gates of the palatial house in Cinnamon Gardens; the grounds were alive with fairy lights and music. Greta tried again to rekindle her anticipation. They left the car to be parked by the servant boy who came forward to greet them, and made their way to the door. The rich hum of voices and laughter told them that the party was well underway.

"It's only seven-thirty. I wonder if they've made their announcement yet?" Greta's sudden glow of excitement hid her nervousness. Few but Jeff would recognise it at all.

His arm encircled her waist. "Let's find Lester and Tilly and see."

Before they had a chance to make their way through the spacious drawing room, now filled with a whirl of colour, people and noise, a large woman approached them barring their way.

She was dressed in an exquisite blue sari and swathed in gold jewellery and perfume.

"Oh no! Joan de Kretser!" Greta attempted to turn away, but Jeff's arm steadied her.

"Too late." His voice was a whisper that only Greta could hear, as he smiled in greeting at the woman in front of them.

"Darlings! You'll never guess what! Sheila's engaged to Jan van Twest and they're off to Canada. Aren't they funny? Having this big party and not wanting any presents." The odour of her perfume mixed with perspiration was suffocating.

Greta thought of Sheila; she could barely remember her from school, had seen almost nothing of her since, and yet the thought of her getting engaged and married and leaving Ceylon in the space of months brought a wave of intense emotion with it. "It's a bit much to take in, isn't it?" Her words were barely audible. Her fear at the impending change in her own life began to overwhelm her newfound resolve on the matter. She struggled to think clearly. She went pale.

With practised assurance Jeff took charge. He steered Greta through the crowd of friends and acquaintances onto a side patio. Here they found an unexpected oasis of coolness and quiet before the party spilled again into the rear gardens, where a band played waltzes and couples glided over the specially laid dance floor. They stood together in silence. Partially obscured by the branches of a large frangipani, they surveyed the scene before them.

"How are we going to do it, Jeff? How are we going to leave?" Her voice wavered, and he felt her body tremble slightly.

"I'm not sure, sweetheart, but we'll find a way." His arm around her hugged her more firmly. He stroked her cheek lightly with his fingers.

"Come on, you two. You'd think you were the new lovebirds, hiding out here by yourselves. You know it's considered indecent to prefer each other's company when you've been married more than a year."

157

Jeff laughed. "What would you know about it, Kingsley? You've shown no sign of ever finding out for yourself." He caught Kingsley's eye and inclined his head ever so slightly. It was enough. Kingsley understood immediately that Greta knew of his plan to leave Ceylon, that it was by now their plan. Greta saw none of this as she took Kingsley's arm and they made their way down the steps to join in the celebrations.

The trio circled the edge of the dance floor and approached an elegant couple who were standing to one side surveying the dancers with pleasure. Jeff moved forward to greet them. "Tilly, Lester, I hear congratulations are in order." He kissed his hostess on the cheek and shook her husband's hand warmly. "So, you'll be losing your baby?" All three laughed lightly, as mixed emotions vied within each. "Where is she, I must congratulate her and her young man in person!" His eyes searched the dance floor.

"Oh, plenty of time for that. Come, let me pick your brains first." Lester began to draw Jeff aside. He was desperate to know the state of play in a boundary dispute Jeff was handling for him.

Greta let go of Kingsley's arm and came to greet her hosts while they were still both present. "Baby"? "Young man"? The words milled around in her head, shocked her. Sheila Leembruggen was, at most, three years younger than her. Yet Jeff saw her so differently. She felt deeply unsettled and fought to steady herself. He had met her at nineteen, seen her as a young woman, while he must have known Sheila since she was a child and he in his early twenties. Yes, that would be different, surely? She was getting confused, she could sense it. She thought of Albert and the way he had treated her. Why? Jeff had never treated her badly. Her head felt muddled again. She fought to clear it, to focus on what was happening around her.

Kingsley was laughing and chatting with Tilly and another couple that Greta didn't know. She stood silently at the periphery of the group longing to leave it. Kingsley looked at her and saw that she was struggling. He felt some pity for her. It was not her fault that Jeff had chosen her. She seemed so hard at times and yet could be so brittle. How were the two of them going to fare, alone with their child in a new country? But, of course, they would not be alone. There would be Ronald; the magnanimous, the ever present, ever capable, to smooth the transition, to comfort them at time of need. His knot of bitterness welled. He had forced himself to come tonight, to play his part. Time to fall into his performance like the trained cur that he was. He smiled and held out his arm. Greta took it with relief and they joined the lively throng on the dance floor.

Greta embraced the dancing and her head began to clear. Kingsley was the most amazing dancer. Just the slightest change in the pressure of his hand on her back and she knew the next direction, the next tight succession of turns that would undoubtedly send them gliding around and away from any possible collision. Jeff was a wonderful dancer, but Kingsley was better. She felt sure that he was attracted to her and she had, on the rarest of occasions, allowed herself to wonder whether he would be as good in bed as he was on the dance floor. It was the closest she ever came to a thought of infidelity and she shied away from it immediately it entered her consciousness. But it made Kingsley special to her. She harboured a strange sense of proprietorship where he was concerned. They shared a deep loyalty to Jeff, that much was clear, yet she felt sure she would always tantalise and disappoint him. It excited her.

She felt enlivened by the music and the couples swirling around her. The dance floor was wonderful, so sheen. The Leembruggens had spared no expense tonight; to announce a new life for their daughter and to bid her farewell. Should she tell Kingsley of their decision? She sensed that it was Jeff's right to do so, and yet she was impatient to know more, to have more. If she could persuade Kingsley to come with them, life in Australia might be more enjoyable, safer at least, surely?

The music quietened to a slow waltz. She looked up at him. "Kingsley? Can I tell you something? It's something that I'm not sure I should tell you." She was subdued, serious. "And when Jeff talks to you about it, it will probably be best to act as if you don't know." She looked away, then back at him.

He smiled. "Go ahead."

"We're leaving, Kingsley, leaving Ceylon. We've just decided. We're going to Australia. Jeff has a friend there, Ronald someone, who's offered him a job."

He kept his face composed. He let an air of sadness linger before he spoke. It was easy. He was so used to acting in her presence. He put as much truth as he could into his lie. "I guess it's not a complete surprise. Everyone's going somewhere. But I'll miss you terribly … both of you."

"Well, that's just it, you don't have to!" She suddenly looked very young. "You can come with us. Then things won't be so different, for any of us." She hesitated for a moment. "You must know this … Ronald? Jeff says he's as good a friend as you. It's so strange he's never mentioned him before, or at least I don't remember anything he's said about him, so he can't have said much!"

So, out of sight, out of mind? Was that to be his fate too, or did Jeff simply limit what he shared with her? She was sometimes clearly threatened by his wide circle of acquaintance, when hers was so small. How much did Jeff keep from her? Had he kept up regular correspondence with Ronald, or merely called on an assumed kinship and loyalty at a time of need? She was looking at him expectantly. "Ah, Ronald de Souza, yes, we were all at school together. He and I never got on that well, though Jeff and he were great friends." He paused. "Thank you, Greta. Thank you for asking. For wanting me to come. But I'm not sure that I'd pass the Australians' racial requirements."

It wasn't strictly true, he most likely would, but it was the most expedient excuse. The thought of leaving his homeland for some colonial backwater was abhorrent to him. His mind was made up. If he could no longer be near Jeff, he would have London and the freedom he might find there. He dared not hope for love; for he still had to let go of the man he had thought of as the love of his life since his early teens. He gave her a rueful smile and continued with complete honesty. "I don't think that I want to go to Australia, or to work with Ronald. I've given this some thought myself. I'll be going to London sometime soon. I'm just not sure when."

Such a simple little speech. Announcing the end of life as he knew it: country, friendship, love, all relegated to a fast approaching past in a few short sentences. He had lost his family and survived. Surely, he would survive this too. He suddenly felt trapped with her. He scanned the garden for Jeff and saw him standing near the far corner of the dance floor by a large purple bougainvillea that had been trained into the shape of a bush. He was deep in conversation with Reggie Kumar.

"I never thought I would hear this from you, Jeff! Didn't realise you were one of those Burghers who just think of themselves as European and forget about any Tamil or Sinhalese blood they have." Reggie's voice was dry and terse. "So, what about the rest of us? Happy to let us sink or swim? I thought you claim to love this country, consider it your own?"

Jeff had never seen his friend so animated. Reggie Kumar had always been the epitome of a civilised man: reliable, calm, a font of knowledge on all things financial and political. Jeff could recall no discord between them as adults, and only the most minor boyhood disagreements from years long past. Reggie had played chess with his grandmother, had frequented his home along with Kingsley and Ronald since boyhood. Jeff had never been on the receiving end of his disapproval in this way. "I didn't think it would affect you so deeply."

Reggie's wife Rita stood beside him. She placed her hand gently on his arm, he turned to her, held her eye for a moment, and nodded. "My apologies, Jeff. I had hoped you would stay. That's all."

161

Jeff looked at his friend and his wife with newfound concern. Reggie was Tamil, Rita was Sinhalese. They were both Christian and from wealthy, well-connected families, whom they had defied in order to marry. One a favourite child, the other an only child, they had managed to maintain their position in each family regardless. They formed a formidable duo. Jeff knew he could not speak of his most compelling reason for leaving: his wish for a different life than the one he foresaw for his child. Their children were in a more precarious situation still, and yet it was now very evident, Reggie would never consider leaving.

It dawned on him, what Reggie said was true; he considered himself Ceylonese, yet he undoubtedly also considered himself European. Until recently the two had not been mutually exclusive. Now they were. He had realised for a long time that his European heritage made it more possible for him to leave, but he now recognised a different and deeper truth: that it also gave him greater freedom to make this choice. His family may have lived here for hundreds of years but his sense of national identity did not reside in this island alone. He failed entirely to acknowledge the true thrust of his friend's anger: his complete emotional denial of the ancestry that bound him to the island for millennia not centuries, and whose place in his make-up and sense of self went unheeded.

Kingsley and Greta appeared beside them. "You all look far too serious!" Kingsley deposited one friend's wife by his side and offered his arm to the wife of the other. "Rita, may I have the pleasure?"

"Of course, Kingsley, I'd love to." Rita turned casually to Greta and kissed her in greeting. "Greta, you look so beautiful in that dress. Did your mother make it for you?"

"Oh no, I have a tailor now!" She was about to say more, but Rita smiled at them all as she took to the dance floor with Kingsley.

Reggie leant forward and kissed Greta as well. "Yes, my dear, that really is your colour." Greta glowed at the compliments.

Reggie looked at his wife gliding away and saw by the sudden laughter in her eyes and smile on her face, that she had rapidly become absorbed in some playful exchange with Kingsley. He turned to Jeff and inclined his head in their direction. "I suppose he's going with you?" His tone was morose.

Greta piped in unexpectedly. "No, he's not." Both men looked at her in surprise. "I hope you don't mind, Jeff, I told Kingsley that we've decided to go. I asked him to join us, but he says he's been thinking about it too, and that he wants to go to London." Her voice was serious and concerned. "He sounded really set on the idea. I'm not sure if you'll be able to change his mind. Though I hope you'll try?"

Jeff felt a surge of gratitude to Kingsley, who had clearly played his part. Greta's acceptance of his decision to leave and choice of destination appeared to be going seamlessly. So strange, he had anticipated enormous difficulty in convincing Greta and there had been none. The task, it seemed, had been done for him by her conversations earlier that day with her friend Sylvia and with her mother. He had not, on the other hand, foreseen any difficulty with two of his lifelong friends, had assumed that his friendship with each would stand the test of any changed life circumstance or separation. Yet, they were both taking the news so badly; each with a different and nuanced response that challenged his credibility in ways he would not have thought possible.

He excused himself and left Reggie to wander off in search of other company as he took to the dance floor with Greta. He would make time to visit Reggie, to talk with him further. But he realised that he would never again see such a spontaneous and honest reaction. Reggie would be polite, understanding, diplomatic, his disappointment and anger cloaked by practised, habitual civility. Perhaps he had been fortunate after all, to have caught his friend unawares at a party, to know what he truly felt about his decision, hard though that may be.

He turned his attention to Greta. Her body was relaxed. She seemed to be enjoying herself. Maybe he could too. A slow waltz began. She leant her head against his shoulder as they moved silently amid this company of their own people, across the silken surface, through the humid warmth of the night. They were leaving, this might never be again; like a refrain that paired with the music, the words circled in his mind. He held her closer. Her unexpected acceptance of his decision left him with no battle to fight, free to feel. He was shocked by the depth of the sadness and longing that enveloped him as he immersed himself in his surroundings; savouring every moment, every aspect of this world, so long taken for granted, now passing. He felt her stroke his arm and looked down at her.

"It will be okay, Jeff. We'll manage. You'll see."

She was reassuring him. How strange and unexpected. He smiled at her but said nothing. The music slowed even further. He held her closer. He felt the full force of it. No matter how compelling the reasons, great courage would be required in the doing of the thing, in the leaving. "You're being so brave."

"I'm trying not to let myself think about anything but the practicalities, not with all these people around!"

"Very wise." He kissed the top of her head. "I think I need to do the same. Do you mind, I have a couple of people I need to have a quick word with? I saw Sylvia Kelly heading for the buffet table. Can I leave you with her for a little while?"

"Jeff, I'm not a child!" Her playful tone belied her gratitude. She knew he would not be gone for long.

They found Sylvia and Greta stayed behind as Jeff began to climb the steps of the patio. He was focused on finding a business associate he had seen head indoors. Someone touched his arm. His body stiffened, and he jerked his arm slightly in shock as he stopped walking.

"Didn't mean to startle you." Kingsley's voice was unusually deep, his enunciation somewhat stilted. "Need to have a word, Jeff, about something important, while I still have the courage."

Anyone else might miss it entirely, but Jeff recognised at once that his friend had been drinking and drinking heavily. It was the only time that his voice sounded this way. He had seen Kingsley in this state on a mere handful of occasions in all the time they had known each other. He hesitated. Was he up to more criticism, let alone drunken recrimination? Yet, despite being deeply shocked by his decision and news, Kingsley had really helped with Greta. He owed him a hearing. "Okay, Kingsley. But I'm on my way to try and catch Carl Myers."

"Ah, an urgent matter then?" Kingsley's voice was laced with sarcasm.

Jeff braced himself. If it was going to be difficult, best have it done. "What is it?"

Kingsley was silent for a moment: dare he speak the truth? There may be no future occasion. But the words that tumbled from his mouth surprised them both. "I'm sorry, Jeff, so sorry that I persuaded you to leave Amy."

"Amy? Kingsley, I don't understand what you're on about! Why, on earth, have you suddenly got this thing about Amy in your head? My memory of it is that you expressed some concerns about her commitment to me, and you were right! I never told you, but I went ahead and asked her to marry me, to come to Ceylon for a year or two until I sorted out my parents' affairs. You know how chaotic I was after they died. I wanted her with me. Told her we could go back to Scotland and make a life there if it didn't work out." He looked at Kingsley who was staring at him in clear surprise at what he was hearing. He went on. "She said no! Couldn't leave her parents. Couldn't leave Scotland."

He stopped. He spoke more slowly, with a quiet certainty. "It was an enormous blow to me at the time. I was barely coping as it was. But it worked out in the end. Don't you know how grateful I am to you for all the support you gave me? … Besides, I wouldn't have found Greta! I wouldn't have Leila! It would have been a different life. One with far more intellect and less passion certainly." He laughed.

"You truly love Greta?" Kingsley sounded incredulous.

"Of course, I love Greta! Why else would I marry her? I feel more alive with Greta than I ever felt with any woman before her. She loves me, she wants me. She may not adore Keats, but she's real!" He stared at Kingsley, then looked away.

Kingsley was broadsided. Even in this, his great betrayal, his belief that he had led Jeff away from the woman he supposed to be the true love of his life, he had been mistaken, had over-estimated his importance. Jeff held no grudge against him at any deeper level. He was even grateful to him for his counsel. He stood staring at the ground. Amy, such a wonderful rare person, relegated to live in memory as someone who adored Keats? What would his place be in time?

"If you'll excuse me, Kingsley."

"What? Yes, yes of course. Carl Myers awaits. Don't let me detain you."

* * *

"So, Sylvie, you were right!" Greta gave her friend a small smile as they stood at the buffet table, carefully selecting choice morsels of food that would not overfill their stomachs or cause any distension or unsightly bulge in their close-fitting dresses.

"Only half right! I had no idea at all about their plans for Canada!" Sylvia was clearly put out at not having been taken into complete confidence on the matter. She still had not approached Sheila Leembruggen or her fiancé to congratulate them in person. It was quite unlike her.

Neither had Greta, but for different reasons. She did not deem it necessary. She was here because of Jeff's relationship

166

with these people and would only extend herself if required to do so while in his company. She had little thought for her hosts once she had relieved herself of her perceived social obligation by greeting them. Instead she was toying with the idea of telling Sylvia her own news. She could see no objection to doing so. Sylvie might be shocked at such a radical change of plan in the few short hours since their last conversation, but she would also be very pleased to be one of the first to find out. Greta waited until they were seated at a table by the dance floor. "Sylvie, I have something to tell you." She looked both flushed and excited. It suddenly felt strangely empowering, to be the one imparting such news, the one about to say goodbye. "We're going too! Jeff and I talked about it on the way here. He's been making some enquiries and we're going to Australia!"

Sylvia stopped eating and put her fork down. She remained silent, staring doggedly at the contents of her plate.

Greta smiled at her friend. "Ridiculous I know, given that I didn't want to hear about anyone else deciding to go there! But Jeff has his reasons, to do with work mostly. It all seems to make sense."

Sylvia looked up. "Oh Greta, not you too! I'm going to end up on my own here. Or left with everyone else's parents." She caught herself and attempted to be conciliatory. "What about your mother? She wouldn't know yet, would she? Maybe she'll go to England now, to be with Cynthie."

"Why would you assume that? We could certainly use some help." Greta's voice was terse. She struggled with her annoyance. Sylvia was one the few people who was her friend in her own right. She softened her tone. "Jeff thinks it's best that she comes with us, and I agree. She and I talked about the state of things here after you left today. She's worried there's going to be a civil war. So, it's better that she doesn't stay."

"A civil war! Surely not!" Sylvia blanched. Emma de Zylva was an intelligent woman, and not prone to idle speculation.

"You two seem very serious! This is a party, come on, cheer up." Frank Kelly and another man had arrived to stand beside them. Frank placed his hand on his wife's shoulder affectionately and bent to kiss Greta in greeting. "Greta my dear, you look beautiful as always. I saw you and Jeff dancing earlier, that dress of yours is very eye-catching."

"One of your mother's creations? You were always so stylish, if memory serves."

The deep male voice was so familiar. Greta's body tensed immediately. A wave of revulsion emanated from her stomach and made its way up her gullet into her throat. She clenched her lips as the nausea hit her. She hesitated. She could not look up, yet she knew she had to. She must somehow behave in an ordinary way, greet him as a man of no consequence, a mere acquaintance from her past.

She lifted her eyes slowly. He looked so much older: balding, greying, his belly protruding. He repulsed her. Even if the sordid things that had happened between them had never occurred, how had she ever found him wonderful or exciting? But they had occurred. He could ruin her in an instant. That was the truth of it. If he told anyone and it got out, what would Jeff think? After years of mingling in society and never encountering him she had thought herself safe, was sure that they must move in completely different circles. Why now, when she was about to leave the island? They had to go, the sooner the better. They had to go. Her thoughts raced. Her heart pounded. She struggled for some semblance of normalcy. "Mr van den Berg."

"Albert, please!" His tone was ingratiating, effusive. "Let's not stand on formality. I understand congratulations are in order since last we met Mrs van Buuren, or may I still call you Greta?"

It was so hard having him standing there, next to Frank, looming over her. She ignored his taunting parry and lowered her eyes. She addressed her next response to a place somewhere to the left of his midriff. "And Mrs van den Berg, is she with you?"

"Oh yes, she's somewhere about." He waved his hand in the general direction of the dance floor with casual irritation.

Before he could go on Greta turned to Sylvia. She needed to give this a context. She had to retain her ability to function, to talk. "She was a customer of my mother's many years ago, when I was at school."

She tried to calm herself, to keep thinking. Yes, she had been a schoolgirl. Yet, if he said anything to anyone about what had happened between them, she would undoubtedly be seen by many as the seductress who had led a married man astray. She was certain that this was the way her sister Cynthia saw her. But the truth of it was that when she knew him she had been sixteen, while he had been in his early forties. Somehow, being with Jeff had helped her grapple with her own self-hatred and recrimination without any conscious effort to do so.

Jeff was ten years older than her and always considerate and thoughtful about any difference this might make between them. She realised with an involuntary shudder that Albert must be at least twenty-five years older than her. He had seen her naivety and used it completely to his own advantage. She had been duped and manipulated. But she couldn't afford to be overwhelmed by the reality of what she was feeling now. She had to find some way to get as far from him as she could without being obvious or raising suspicions.

"May I have this dance, Greta?" Albert was holding out his hand to her.

Did he think he could still bend her to his will? He must be mad, had to be. Fortunately, she was with Sylvia and Frank Kelly; two of the most trusting and guileless people she knew. "I'm afraid I'm not up to any more dancing, Mr van den Berg, excuse me." She turned to Sylvia. "I need to go to the powder room, Sylvie, come with me?" She hoped her voice wasn't trembling. She could feel that her legs were. With Sylvia's help

169

she might get away, feign illness once gaining the sanctuary of the bathroom and have Jeff brought to her. They could leave. She had to leave, this party, this country.

"Of course, Greta." Sylvia and Greta rose at the same time and Sylvia took Greta's arm.

Albert stepped forward suddenly and seized Greta by her other arm. "Are you sure, Greta? We may not get this chance again."

Greta yelped softly as she pulled her arm abruptly from his grasp. She took a few rapid steps away from him and Sylvia came with her.

Sylvia turned to both men and gave them conciliatory looks over her shoulder. "Excuse us, it's been a very big day. I'll tell you about it later, Frank."

They made their way to the bathroom far more slowly than Greta would have liked, but there was no hurrying her trembling legs, no silencing the pounding of her heart in her ears. Sylvia realised that her friend was not well. She helped her cautiously up the steps to the patio and into the house. She scanned the large lounge room for Jeff, as she negotiated their way to the bathroom with brief nods and smiles in the direction of acquaintances encountered along the way.

"Here we are, Greta. Will you be alright by yourself? I've never seen you look so pale. I really think I should find Jeff."

"I'm feeling dreadful. I'm not sure why." She pushed the bathroom door open and turned. "Please find Jeff, we'd best head home."

"At least you had the chance to dance before this came on. It must be too much excitement. Such a huge decision. I still can't believe you'll be going." Sylvia's eyes began to fill with tears and she hurried away.

Greta was hugely relieved to enter the bathroom and be alone. She locked the door and stared into the mirror in front of her. She looked drawn, pale, frightened. She splashed cold water on her face and patted it dry with the hand towel.

She pinched her cheeks and looked again. A wave of nausea caught her suddenly; she hurried to the toilet and bent over it. She began to retch but nothing came up. The retching continued, surge after surge. Finally, she vomited up a little food followed by clear liquid. She stood with her head over the toilet bowl until she was sure it had finished, then cleaned the top of the bowl with toilet paper and flushed the toilet. She washed her hands, rinsed her mouth, and patted her face dry once more.

Jeff came to her soon after she emerged from the bathroom. She was seated on a sofa in one corner of the crowded lounge, looking very pale. "I'm so glad I found you. Sylvia told me you're not well." He sat down beside her as he spoke. He looked so concerned. He stroked her hair gently. Then his expression turned suddenly to one of deep distaste. "I was on my way back to you when Edna Misso stopped me and told me that something unpleasant had happened between you and Albert van den Berg. Are you alright? Do I need to talk to him?"

"No, no it was nothing. He wanted to dance, but I couldn't because I felt sick. I just hurried off. I didn't want everyone to know."

"I have no idea what he's doing here. The man has the most unsavoury reputation. I can't stand the thought of him being anywhere near you." He was silent for a moment. "Do you know him?"

She caught her breath. She tried to talk as calmly as she could. "I met him once at Inez and Edward's house, many years ago, when I was still at school. My mother made a few dresses for his wife shortly after that." She had to stop this conversation now. She could not risk giving herself away. He knew her too well. "Jeff, please take me home. I'm not well. I don't want to talk about that man anymore."

"Of course, darling, of course. I'll have them bring the car to the door. I'll only be a moment."

They drove in silence most of the way home. The warmth of the air felt cloying to her now, but the breeze played with her

171

hair once again and brought some relief. She leant her head against the back of the seat and closed her eyes. She felt terrified by the possibilities that raced in her mind. If someone had taken the trouble to find Jeff and tell him of her altercation with Albert, then how many people had seen it? What had they seen? What would they surmise? What if someone thought to ask Albert? After all these years of silence, would he give her away? Might her rudeness to him tonight provoke spite or revenge? Her head began to ache and spin. She had to stop thinking about it.

Jeff looked at her. She looked so pale. Had he been foolish to confront her with his plans on the way to the party as he had? Was this sudden news too much for her? She had seemed so taken with it in her own way. Perhaps she was overexcited. He must proceed with their plans more carefully. Let the idea continue to percolate over the days to come. He had a sudden image of the scene described by Edna Misso: Albert van den Berg grabbing Greta's arm and Greta pulling away from him. He felt a surge of anger followed by something quite different. The man was a known lecher. But she had said she knew him as the merest of acquaintances. He pushed suspicion of anything else from him. They had enough to contend with without unwarranted fears, or succumbing to innuendo about his wife, especially from such an unreliable, or more likely vindictive, source.

He pulled up in front of their porch and brushed the hair from her face. She opened her eyes. She looked so fragile, so lovely. He regretted any glimmer of suspicion he may have harboured. He climbed out of the car, came around to her door and opened it for her. He held his hand to her and helped her out. She took his arm as she walked gingerly in her high heel shoes on the gravel of the driveway. She swayed slightly, and he put his arm around her waist to steady her. He led her indoors and to their bedroom. He helped her to remove her jewellery and she began to undress. He brought her nightgown to her

172

and watched as she slipped it over her head. She climbed into their bed and he kissed her forehead as he covered her with the sheet. "I'll join you shortly, sweetheart. I'll just check on Leila first and I think I need a moment or two by myself."

He left their bedroom and Greta pulled his pillow to her. She lay on her side and curled her body around it. She began to shake. She sobbed silently until she heard his footsteps receding, then something in her snapped; her breathing came in short rapid gasps, her body shook convulsively, she wanted to cry out, but muffled any sound by biting into the pillow she was clutching. The memory of Albert's hand gripping her arm repulsed her. What if he tried to contact her? How could she leave their house again? They had to leave this country, as soon as possible. They had to go.

Jeff found Charlotte asleep on the floor of his daughter's bedroom. She stirred as he entered the room, sat up and looked at him without speaking. "Thank you, Charlotte. You can go to bed now." She was surely just roused from sleep, but her face was sombre, her expression different to any he could recall. She nodded wordlessly and left. He remembered suddenly that Greta had behaved oddly earlier in the day, had been so rude to Charlotte that it seemed she might not stay. Perhaps this idea of leaving had been upsetting Greta all day. He hoped that things might settle more as they planned their departure. He needed Charlotte to stay until then. They all did.

Once she left he walked further into the room and stood looking down at his daughter. She lay fast asleep, her mass of golden brown curls encircled her face. He kissed her forehead tenderly then sank to sit at the foot of her bed. How was it possible that Greta could not love this wonderful little being, her own daughter? Why had he so readily ignored the harshness in her behaviour to their child? How would they cope without an ayah? Would Emma be able to take her place? He bent forward and let his head rest in his hands. He felt the room spin. Perhaps he had drunk too much whisky.

He rose, steadied himself and walked slowly through the silent house. As he neared their bedroom he heard a strange gasping, mewing sound, like a child in pain or a young wounded animal. He found her curled in a foetal position, clutching a pillow to her, shaking and crying. He sat beside her and reached out to touch her. She shivered violently as his hand rested on her arm, but she did not shake it off. He let it stay there. Her shaking began to quieten until eventually it ceased. He climbed onto the bed beside her and sat up against the bedhead. She laid her head on his chest. He stroked her hair gently. "What is it, Greta? What is upsetting you?" She made no answer. He continued, his tone placating, his words measured. "We can slow this all down if we need to. I'm happy to consider other options. I'll get in touch with Ronald and let him know. We can talk about it again in the morning." He felt her body stiffen.

She sat up and looked at him strangely. Her voice was trembling, her tone urgent. "No, Jeff, no! We mustn't delay. We have to go, as soon as we can." She stared at him with a pleading look he had never seen from her before, never thought to see.

"Greta, what happened tonight? Is there something I need to know?" He looked at her, but she had averted her eyes. "Greta, you can tell me … anything."

She turned to face him. She looked cornered, trapped, fear flitted in her eyes but suddenly her expression hardened, and she glared at him with a strange ferocity. "Why would you say such a thing? Nothing happened! Nothing's the matter!" She was almost shrieking. She stopped herself, then went on more quietly. "I'm overtired that's all. Perhaps I ate something too rich." But her tone was harsh, her voice icy. She had never spoken to him in this way. She hesitated briefly once more, then began to speak with increasing agitation. "We've made our decision. There's no turning back. We leave, as soon as possible! I'll tell Mum in the morning. Of course she'll come!

174

You're right, she's besotted with Leila." There was hatred in her voice.

He looked at her in shocked silence, for in that moment he did not recognise her as the wife he loved. A question came to him unbidden, unwelcome: could Greta survive this change, would they make it in Australia? But he must put such thoughts behind him. He could not afford to give them credence. There was too much to do.

GLOSSARY

Almirah—free-standing cupboard or wardrobe, usually large and made of wood

Arrack—distilled alcohol from *toddy* (coconut sap)

Ayah—nanny

Kadalei—also known as kadala, Sinhalese way of cooking split peas and other pulses with chilli and spices, sold fried or dry-roasted in twisted paper cones by street vendors

Dhobi—man or woman who launders and irons clothing and linen

DBU—Dutch Burgher Union

"Eyata yanna denna!"—"Let her go!" in Sinhalese

Jungies—little girls' underpants

Kondai—Sinhalese term for hair in a bun; a hairstyle worn by both men and women

Lamprais—Burgher dish comprising parcels of rice, curries, sambal, and meatballs wrapped in banana leaves and baked in an oven

Perahera—(procession), the Kandy Perahera is a religious festival to pay homage to the Tooth Relic of the Buddha. Lavishly adorned elephants form an important part of the procession

Raththaran baba—golden baby, a Sinhalese term of deep endearment

Sambal—condiment served to accompany rice and curry, often containing coconut, chillies, onions and lime

Vesak—the day commemorating the birth, the enlightenment and the death of the Buddha

Peterites—boys who attend St Peter's College

ACKNOWLEDGEMENTS

This is a work of fiction; all the characters in it and the events of their lives are fictious. However, the story is placed in a historical setting, where real events occurred. I am grateful for two outstanding texts as sources for my research; *Proud and Prejudiced: The Story of the Burghers of Sri Lanka* by Rodney Ferdinands, and *People Inbetween* by Michael Roberts et al.

With thanks to:

My mother, Vilma Schokman, for her first-hand knowledge of working for the British military during the Second World War.

My aunt, Dorothy Van Twest, for her wonderful descriptions of Colombo in the 1940s, 50s, and 60s, including the restaurants, night clubs and bands of any era.

Ishara Senadheera for her help with Sinhalese words and phrases.